Figs

& Pomegranates

& Special Cheeses

A Love Story

MONA GUSTAFSON AFFINITO

Figs & Pomegranates & Special Cheeses

First Printing August 2014
Copyright © 2014 Mona Gustafson Affinito, Ph.D., L.P.

Books by the author may be ordered through booksellers, including
amazon.com, directly from the author, through
www.monagustafsonaffinito or www.forgivenessoptions.com,
or at forgivenessoptions@earthlink.net

Because of the dynamic nature of the Internet,
any Web addresses or links contained in this book may have changed
since publication and may no longer be valid.
The views expressed in this work are solely those of the author.

ISBN–13: 978-0692257883
ISBN–10: 0692257888

Printed in the United States of America

Print copies available at http://createspace.com
Printed by CreateSpace, An Amazon.com Company

The author:
Mona Gustafson Affinito | forgivenessoptions@earthlink.net

Cover and book design:
Janson Graphics LLC | jansongraphics.com

Watercolor artwork:
Marilyn J. Brown | Wayzata, MN Artist and Illustrator

Photo of the author:
Dan Magnuson Studios | danmagnuson.com

Contents

In Appreciation

"Figs & Pomegranates & Special Cheeses" is the re-edited and re-titled offspring of "Mrs. Job," the fictional story of the wife of biblical Job. I'd like, therefore, to thank all those who helped me understand the theology and lessons of the Book of Job. Detailed appreciation is included in the Addendum section at the end of the book.

Thanks go as well to Jay Johnson's father, Stu Johnson, who devoted the last years of his life to enthusiastically researching and sharing background information on the environment and life of Job's time.

Finally, in addition to the recognitions in the end section of the book, I want to thank two women who assisted in the birth of this new version as if they were loving co-parents. Marilyn Brown whose water color art was the basis for the cover, and Jenny Janson who wrapped it all in special enhancements.

To my family of origin

who encouraged in-depth dinner table discussions

of religion, the English language, current events,

and whatever else seemed important.

Thanks Jennie and Carl, Harvey, and Thelma.

"Oh Dara, I did feel that way about your father when we first married, but love changes over time. I guess you could say at first it is like **feasting on figs and pomegranates and special cheeses,** *and later it is like enjoying the evening potage. The thrill may not be so great later on, but each day it fills the empty hole that would be hunger if you did not have each other."*
(p. 50)

1

The End

I will never be Dara again. Only Job remained who had the privilege to address me by my first name, honoring the wisdom it signified. Dara lives no more.

It has been three days since I saw Job for the last time, and touched him, his cold, stiffened, lifeless body invading mine through my ministering fingers. I am enveloped by the mingled odors of the precious oils with which we anointed him -- the sweet smell of lilies of the field, the tenderness of Spikenard, the death-message of myrrh, the tangy odor of cedar and the acrid truth of my own body's anguish. I am shrouded by the vision of his linen-wrapped body on the cold burial slab.

I want to remember my Job alive, but only his mute, icy heaviness touches my recollection. The magnificence of the massive tomb that once reflected and magnified the sun cannot now conceal the truth of his death. We had thought it beautiful with its immense blocks of pale yellow sandstone, several stories high, fronted by engraved copper pillars embossed with gold and silver. Now I see piles of bitter sand, attempts to make something beautiful out of that which is only rotting flesh.

If I could wrap myself around his warmth one more time. But he is locked away behind the heavy bronze gate fronting the tomb. And he is cold. Even the yellow, jasmine, rose and royal purple blooms around the tomb scald my eyes with their mockery. I will never see or feel him again. Those pungent, costly oils assault my nostrils with rancid decay. Did we really believe they could sweeten the putrefaction of death? The once magnificent tomb signifies nothing. My life signifies nothing.

For the past three days my children have attended me. This morning Jemimah,[1] the oldest of my three surviving daughters, awakened me.

How beautiful she is, with her light olive skin and dark eyes, so lovely she never has to enhance her appearance with malachite and red ochre. How proud Job is of her beauty, of the beauty of all three of his daughters.

Filled with joy, I reached for Job to share this moment, and found only emptiness beside me. Then I remembered why she is here. Job is dead. I collapsed onto my couch, yielding in weakness to the distended barrenness of my own ghostly core.

I heard Jemimah as if from a great distance. "Mother, you must get up and prepare yourself to sit with those who are here to grieve with you."

I was hardly aware of dressing, or being dressed. I let my daughters draw me into my royal purple robes, enhanced only by the long flowing sleeves signifying my position as Job's wife. I ate because Jemimah and her sisters insisted I must. The wheat bread might as well have been the barley loaf of the poor since to my taste it was only dried clay.

Then my children's presence bore me like a mindless, obediently-resisting child from our personal quarters to return to the audience hall to sit in mourning for another day.

Our gilded great hall is no longer beautiful to me, but a huge cavern reflecting the bleak hollow of my own emptiness. The purple that once signified our royalty is now muddy gray to my eyes, and the shining gold is nothing but brown rust. I see the inlays of turquoise and cornelian in the floor. Where is their luster now? The purple hangings interspersed about the hall sag in grief. There are the gold statues signifying Job's royal status, directing my eyes to the empty throne to suffer anew the pangs of discovering his absence. There are the carved bas-reliefs honoring the memories of our first family of ten children. My heart constricts with an old agony. Had I really been able to view those memorials without pain? I look around and see all these embellishments melt away like mud into colorless palls of mourning.

So many have come here to be with us in our grief, some out of love for Job and me and our family, many out of duty to Job's position, several paid to sing dirges in honor of the king. Finding no solace, I sink deeper into my own despair.

None of these who are here can truly share in my grief. They will return to their own homes, resuming their own activities, leaving me alone to mourn the death of Job, the death of my life's purpose, the death of Dara. Even my children and my grandchildren will be leaving. Jemimah and her sisters and brothers are so solicitous of me, but they must depart soon. They have their own families to care for. I remember how it is to mourn with friends and relatives, then to return home to resume one's normal life. That will not happen for me. I can see only nothingness ahead.

Some here have known me long enough to remember the trials Job and I endured years ago, but that pain, returning so agonizingly for me now, is a distant memory for them.

Strange how this present anguish sweeps the past in with it. Then I wanted to scream and moan, but I could not. I had to bury that unspeakable pain; I was too busy. So much depended on me to see that the dead were buried, the living fed, and all were comforted.

There was responsibility then, and even hope. All was lost, but my Job was still alive. And, indeed, Job's God - our God - kept his promises. But life cannot last forever. Now

I am not fighting the torment. I am numb. Our story, my story, is over. I am the past. I am gone.

I cannot give in to this despair. I must summon the will to meet my new responsibilities. It will be different now. It is too soon even to know who will take Job's place as king. It will probably be our eldest son, but the Council of Elders will make the final decision. I do not even want to think about that. Now that Job is dead, I will have no position as a leader of the kingdom.

I do not want to go on without Job. I want to give up. Maybe I would like to die. It has been a very long road.

Suddenly I am aware of the constant hum of coming and going, and the wailing of the official mourners. A wave of movement is spreading through the room. Jemimah is whispering to me.

"Mother, there is an old servant woman approaching – boldly, as if we should know her, as if she has a right to come at us like this."

At first I gaze empty-eyed at this woman in brown nomad linen. Then grey coils of hair, springing defiantly out from under her headscarf, stab deep into my body, unlatching a long-protected memory. It is Adah, on her knees now.

"Dara," she says. Then, as in a ritual, "Forgive me, forgive me, forgive me."

I stop breathing, tears erupting as I plummet into the past. The crowds around me become the hustle and bustle of our tribe. My childhood home becomes the only reality for me now. The tears I could not shed for Job become a sobbing, gasping wailing as I run in memory to my mother, who is sitting with one of my aunts cross-legged at the hand mill in our tent, crushing the barley grain into flour.

"Adah pulled the hair off my doll's head."

I am a little girl again, heartsick that the beautiful lengths of yarn strung with quartz beads have been ripped off my doll's pottery head. Even worse, Adah stands behind me, tugging on my outer garment as she whispers in my ear, trying too late to stop me from telling what she did. I want my mother to scold her, maybe even give me permission to pull the hair-beads out of Adah's doll. Of course, she does not.

"Dar', you know Adah is your best friend. You two will find a way to restore good feelings."

I do not want to. I want to hate her forever. Stamping my feet, I push her out toward her own tent. "Go away. I want never to play with you again." I am glad she is crying. Crawling, shaking, and sobbing, making sure my mother sees how awful this is, I search for the pink, blue, and violet hair beads until I find them all, throwing them one at a time into a pile on the edge of the rug.

"Here, Dar', give them to me. I will string them on new lengths of yarn for you and boil you some hide glue so you can reattach them to your doll's head."

I throw the beads into my mother's lap, grab the broom, and bend over to sweep the dirt floor of the tent. I have already done it once this morning, but I need to do something angry. It is hard work, and I can complain to myself that Adah is ruining my life. Trying not to be calmed by the many pretty colors of broomcorn tied together with stiff flax rope, I swish it even faster and harder. Even that angry satisfaction is limited as my mother scolds.

"Be careful. You are stirring up too much dust. It will get into the barley we are grinding."

I jab a few more swishes, then put the broom down. I am trying to stay mad, but my eyes are filling with tears and my insides are starting to hurt in a different way.

What shall I do? I want to be with Adah, but I cannot

13

pretend she has done nothing wrong. I want to play with Adah. But I want to stay mad at her.

So how is it that I find myself outside again, pulling my blue head covering up for protection from the sun, and calling to her to come and play? I am not surprised that she is nearby, waiting to be with me.

I feel all warm again, wanting to hug her, but not wanting her to know I am not still mad. I cannot help myself. I like how it feels to be with her – safe, the way things are supposed to be.

Sometimes after we have made up from a fight I look at her very carefully, like I have not seen her for a while. Her hair causes me to smile. It looks like the desert making waves in the bright sun of the middle of the day, but maybe a little more like it has been caught in a sandstorm. No matter how she tries, she cannot stop it from springing out from under her headscarf. I do not like to confess it, but I am jealous of those curls, and of her cinnamon skin that sometimes has little specks of iron in it, especially when she is excited. Mostly, though, I like the way her quiet, olive eyes make me feel calm.

I am so different. People say we are too opposite to be such good friends. Instead of curls, I have long, thick black hair that pops back into ripples when someone pulls it. My bronze skin with no extra flecks of anything looks quiet, but that is not how I am. My mother tells me the blackness of my eyes sometimes makes me look like I am stabbing someone with them. I do not like that. I would rather look like Adah, or at least be as tall as she is.

At first, we approach sideways. I want her to say she is sorry. But it does not seem to matter anymore. We grasp each other's hands and run to pick some carob. All is calm again as we suck its sweetness.

We were best friends. Out of all the children in our camp, she was the special one. We played; we fought; we made up and fought again. We daydreamed; we made believe we were grown up. We pretended we were brides; we imagined we were mothers. We tried rouging our faces and enhancing our eyes with powdered malachite and red ochre when our sisters let us beg some from them. When we could not have the real thing, we pretended to make some with sand and oil. We played with each other's hair, making hers spring back when I pulled on it and mine fall into and out of waves when it was touched. We held each other when we were scared. We got into trouble together, like the time we offered Astarte, our household goddess, a sacrifice of a little sheep that we had formed out of mud.

"How dare you treat Astarte that way," my mother irately reprimanded as she gently cleaned off the goddess and kissed her devotionally. "And besides, you have made a mess. Now you clean it up."

That was not the first time, nor the last, that together Adah and I angered and, I suppose, hurt our mothers.

Adah and I imagined all kinds of things together, but we never made believe we were old. Yet here we are now, two old ladies, as if we had never been apart, yet separated forever. My memory is bringing color back to me, the reds, yellows, and blues of the rug on our dirt floor and the mingled oranges and greens in the material waiting for my mother to return to the loom.

Adah's coming has released my anguish and restored me to life at the same time. I want to forgive her. I want to fall on my knees and embrace her. I do not know. Maybe I have. It is all a blur.

2

The Beginning

Adah helped me attach the new strings of beads to my doll's head.

"Let us come back after the glue dries and oil our dolls. We can pretend the water jar is filled with oil."

Oiling ourselves protected us from lice and the drying heat of the sun, so of course we had to do the same for our dolls.

"We should not use that water, Dara. We will get in trouble."

"We can use just a little bit. No one will ever notice."

The blue ceramic jug held the water that was caught and saved when the family poured it over our hands before eating. It would be used later to boil the ingredients to dye the materials for my family's weaving. Little as we were, we knew that water was so precious it could cause wars. Everyone knew the stories of nomads being attacked by other tribes trying to drive them away from their wells.

Adah and I had been very little the first time we knew there were bad people out there who might hurt us. Adah noticed it first, the way our camp suddenly seemed to crackle.

"Dar', look! Who are those strange men riding into camp? Look at those golden camels!"

My eyes snapped at the sight of their bright red, orange, blue, and green fabric coverings. "Look at all the donkeys they are leading. Look at all the boxes and bags they are carrying. What do you think is in them?"

It is not true that we had never seen such colorful camels

and heavily laden donkeys before. But this time there were so many at once, and so unexpected.

We had just put our dolls to nap on the little rugs my mother had made for them, and were tucking our unbleached linen robes up under our knees and into our waist bands so we could talk the boys into letting us play Crown the King with them. They had traced a circle in the ground and were about to take turns throwing a die to see how many steps they could take around it. The first one to make it back to the beginning was the king.

"We want to play with you."

"Go away," one of them pretended to push us away with his hands.

"Go play with your dolls or something," another said, folding his arms together as if he were rocking a baby. It made me mad the way he acted like we were silly little girls.

"Leave us alone. Can you not see we are playing Crown the King?"

"We want to have fun too. Do you think we cannot throw the die? Just let us show you."

"Do not be silly. Girls cannot be king."

I put my hands on my hips and yelled, "Of course we can!" And I believed it.

They laughed, winking at each other and pointing fingers toward us.

"Do not laugh at us. You will be sorry if you do," I hollered, feeling my arms get tight and hard, and my fingers curl in stiff on themselves, making my palms hurt in a good kind of way.

They just turned away from us and threw the die.

Would it not be fun to jump into the middle of all of them and keep swinging around until I had knocked them all down?

I might have followed through on my thoughts, even

though I was almost crying at the same time. Adah looked like she was feeling the same way. We should have learned that we would not be allowed to play with the boys, and I guess we would have lost the fight if the boys hit back. They would not have done that though, because being two or three years older than we, they already knew that boys were supposed to protect girls.

Anyway, about the strangers. There were many people in our settlement, so the commotion began to attack our ears like a fight between tall squeals and squat rumbles when the men rode in. The boys who had been playing stood at attention, as if they were heroes who were going to protect the camp. Adah and I, grasping each other's hands, rushed to pick our dolls up from their naps. Holding them tight in our arms, we stood for a while, swinging back and forth, trying to decide whether to go back to the boys or run home to our mothers for protection. Shaking from fear and excitement all at the same time, we looked at each other and then, without a word, ran to Adah's tent. I hugged her mother's right leg and Adah grabbed the left. Her mother, smiling a bit, reached down to touch us on our shoulders.

"Do not worry. These men are not Chaldeans. They have probably taken a sojourn off the King's Highway to find rest from their travels. It might even be fun for you to enjoy their visit."

I looked sideways at Adah. She seemed calmer.

I guess if Adah is not afraid, I should not be either.

Her mother freed our hands from her legs and moved toward her cooking pot. Adah and I reached for each other's hands. We felt safer that way, safe enough to move slowly out of the tent, closer to the crowds outside.

Things began to happen so fast we had no time to wonder if we were still afraid. At first all the grown-ups gathered around the visitors, talking so much we could not even pick out what they were saying. The women were rushing to and fro from their tents, creating waves of color in their bright headscarves donned in honor of the guests, carrying out their best blue, and sometimes pink, ceramic drinking jars filled with water to offer the newcomers. First the men splashed water on their faces and poured some over their hands before they drank until their thirst was gone, using their right hands as cups. Then beer was offered in a large pottery ladle that the men passed around from one to the other.

Our camp felt like a sudden desert storm as the women began bustling about a common fire pit, preparing a huge pot, bigger than what we used just for our own family. The red, orange, and blue flames sent up ripples of heat as they attacked the potage vessel from below. Most of the women, it seemed, were running back and forth, adding lentils and vegetables to the stew. Somehow a few people even came up with the flesh and bones of freshly killed birds. By this time, Adah and I were rushing back and forth too, first putting our dolls back to nap, and then just racing around. There began to appear plates of yellow cheese, fresh golden figs and dried brown ones, purple grapes, black raisins, and red pomegranates, some opened to reveal their crimson berries. There were carob beans to suck on as sweet treats, and almonds and pistachio nuts. Honey and grape juice boiled down to syrup were even provided to spread on bread. We had never seen so much wonderful food at one time. It certainly did not look like we were a poor tribe.

In the meantime, the men of our tribe sat themselves cross-legged in a huge circle with the visitors, exchanging stories and news, talking all at once in one loud rumble. Adah and I slowed down to creep closer to them, trying to hear what they were saying, until our mothers came and took us away.

"That is men's business," they told us

We moved a little bit, just far enough to whisper to each other without being heard.

"Adah," I was shaking all over now. "They said some people were attacked and killed."

"I know. They had to run away from their camp, away from their well."

"And they said their animals were forced to run away, and some were even killed."

Adah and I were both feeling like our bodies were out of our control, so of course we were getting annoyed with each other.

"I heard it too. Do you think my ears do not work? You are not the only one who listened to them."

I guess we would have let our fear lead us into arguing with each other, but just then my mother came back to us.

"Go fetch the tray of cheese that I prepared to bring to our guests. Then see if you can help some of the other women carry their food."

My mother could see I was frightened, so she put me to work. That did help a little. She seemed to know that doing something useful would calm me down. Adah and I ran back and forth, delivering food to the group of men.

When it came time to eat, the guests went first, dipping into the potage with pieces of the flat bread that appeared, like all the other food, out of the nearby tents. All that food and all the special activities helped me forget my terror. I was shuddering with excitement. I had no idea then how much more there would be for the three days the visitors would stay.

On the second day of the visit, they slaughtered a sheep.

I knew that was a very special thing to do, but my stomach lurched and cramped when I saw the fresh red blood spurting from the animal. The warm, sickly sweet smell of the gore made my throat squeeze and squirm so I had to hold myself tight to keep everything inside me. It was not at all like seeing the jars of blood stored quietly along with the containers of urine used for dying fabrics. I did not like the swarms of flies that gathered around the carcass, either. I began to itch all over. But I did calm down and enjoy it when I was given a piece of the roasted meat. That was a special treat; often there was not enough left over for the children after the men and then the women had feasted.

I was afraid again when the strangers slept in our tent the first night, right on the rug in the corner where our whole family usually slept. This night I was with my mother and a couple of my aunts in the women's tent, not in the usual close protection of my father and older brothers. I kept waking up, partly because I was so excited, partly because I could not help thinking someone might try to kill us. I had taken Astarte to bed with me to protect me, though I was a little afraid my parents would not like it if they found out. But her huge breasts and round belly felt good. I knew my mother goddess watched over me, stronger than my mother and Adah's mother and all the mothers of the camp put together.

When I stretched awake in the morning, there was no one beside me to touch. Everyone was up, calmly trying to do their usual morning chores, except that my father did not go out to tend the animals, but stayed instead with the guests. I sneaked Astarte back to her place of honor. If anyone saw me, they did not say anything.

Everyone started the day the same way, folding something inside a piece of bread, like olives, cheese, or dried fruit. And there was lots of it, what with all that was left over from the feast of the day before. My brothers, who were going out to put in their time tending the herds, took some to eat on the way, and the other men from the tribe, who joined my father, had their share too. The men squatted in a circle on our bright red, orange, and blue rug, eating and talking as if they had never stopped from the night before. I folded dried fruit into some flatbread and stood in a corner watching for a while.

The women in my family, dressed in their special blue sashes and head coverings, did their best to keep doing their daily activities. It was a little hard sweeping around the men, but the tent had to be kept clean. My mother and one of her sisters began to crush the grain into flour with the hand mill. We usually ate barley bread, but today they prepared the more precious wheat. My mother mixed the milled flour with water and put some of the previous day's dough into a portion of it to let it stand by the heat of the fire until it rose. The rest she just spread out on a dish over the fire, letting it come out flat. That is how she got the thin slices we used to scoop the evening meal out of the common pot.

But the women were not just doing their chores. They were also working close enough to the men to hear what they were saying. I did not go looking for Adah that morning. Listening to the conversation seemed much more interesting. They talked about people carrying copper from the mines and merchants coming by with fine oils and pottery. They seemed to think that was good news.

I did not understand all of it, but I knew I could ask my father to explain it to me later. Not all the fathers were like mine, but he made sure he taught us all he could, both his sons and his daughters. Of course, my mother was our most important teacher because she was the one we were with most of the time. Even my brothers, when they were very little, spent a lot of time with my mother, doing things like sweeping the floor. But I think maybe my father cared especially for me, the youngest daughter. He was always willing to pull me into his lap when he was sitting. In fact, sometimes I think he squatted down just so he could hold me. This morning, though, he was not paying attention to me.

The excitement of the strangers' visit did wear off. Three days is a long time to remain close to the men, even though the feasting was a delight. On the other hand, I did not want to go too far away. I did not want to miss anything, and, to tell the truth, I was still a little afraid. So I stayed with the women and worked at teasing and stripping fleece, removing burrs and dirt, and separating it into fibers to get it ready for washing, dyeing, and spinning. Carding wool was really a hard job. Even my brothers were expected to do it before they were old enough to go out to work with the men. It was a task that did not require much attention or thinking once it had become routine with practice, so for now it was perfect for listening.

My mother busied herself with spinning wool, twisting it into a kind of string and winding it onto a stick, hovering close to the men while she worked. This time she was twining different colors together: blue, yellow, and red, in a heavy thickness to be used for weaving decorative and warm hangings. In our family, spinning and weaving were a specialty. We were known for making colorful fabrics, some crafted into loose textures for clothing, others heavier for blankets and hangings, and even denser ones for rugs. My mother and her family were skilled not only in dyeing and weaving, but also in creating yarns and threads of different textures and thicknesses. No two patterns were ever alike so each product, although it took hard work, was also somewhat fun to create.

Eventually the time came when the guests were sent on their way with packages of food and a good supply of water. Then I could ask my father to explain why they had stayed with us for so long. That is when I first learned the law of hospitality. My older brothers and sisters had already been through visits from outsiders, so what my father had to say was not new to them. But my body pushed me from inside to relive and understand what had happened. I knew it was important when he sat down and drew me close to sit in that cozy V formed by his crossed legs on the floor.

"Do not ever forget what I will tell you now, Dar'. Every nomad needs to understand the importance of hospitality. It is as important as being safe in our tent at night to sleep."

"Why? What is hospitality, anyway?"

"Hospitality is the way to look after ourselves. It serves to keep people from attacking us. It keeps things peaceful. When strangers come by, we offer them water, food, and a place to rest. That is just the way things are."

"But why did they have to sleep right in our tent – right where I usually sleep with all of you? I didn't like that. I was frightened."

"We do not hold them at a distance, but rather we treat them like members of our tribe. That is why they slept in our tent – as one family. We expect the same treatment when we travel about. Our nomadic life is hard, Dara. Knowing we can be assured of food and a place to stay means we do not have to be afraid of dying of starvation, thirst, and exposure when there are people around who can help. It is really important to promote mutual respect and fair treatment. That, my little one, is what hospitality is all about."

My mother had been nearby, listening, and now she made her way into the conversation. "Besides, Dara, did you not have fun getting to know new people?"

"I guess that is true. I was afraid when they first came, but by the time they left, my fear was gone."

"It is hard," my father said, "to be afraid of people with whom you have shared food, sleeping quarters, and conversation. So, what we said to each other is not the most important thing. What matters is that we were together."

"But what if they were bad people?" I was still afraid of the idea of strangers, even if I had started to feel safe with the men who had just been here.

"The law of hospitality still applies. We cannot turn someone out to starve or die of exposure. But we do not have to endanger ourselves either. So, we feed the enemy, but in a corner away from us, and give him space to sleep, but not with the family, and one of the men is assigned to keep watch."

That explanation made me feel better, but my body was still not all warm and cozy. I suppose I was too good at finding things to worry about. I was satisfied, though, and ran out to tell Adah what I had learned.

Visits from strangers were not the only excitement at our camp. Every once in a while the members of the Council of Elders would ride in, swaying in their canopied seats atop the brightly colored blankets protecting their camels' backs from the press of the acacia wood platforms. I liked it when they came to our camp to gather with my father. It was better than when he traveled away to the meetings. I missed him when he was gone, for one thing, but I also liked it when all my uncles came. They were not all really my uncles, but in our tribe we were all related by membership, even if not through close blood lines.

I particularly loved Zerah Ben Ruel, though. He let me call him Uncle Ruel and he paid special attention to me, because I belonged to my father, I guess. In fact, he usually brought me some special little gift. One time it was an imported miniature indigo pottery container of aromatic oil, having the sweet, fresh scent of the pink rock rose. It made almost all my senses feel good, with the gentle touch of the oil, the scent, and the thought-picture of the plant itself, so lovely with its tiny pale lilac flower spreading out around its center of orange. The vial did not contain enough to replace the oil we used every morning to comb through our hair and wash our bodies. It was meant for my doll. He brought me two of them.

"Give one to that little girl you play with so much. The one who seems to be your best friend."

Adah jumped up and down when she knew there was one for her doll too. "That Uncle Ruel must be really rich."

I had to admit I had not noticed, maybe because I was accustomed to those special favors. Another time he brought me an ivory bracelet. The touch of it was so smooth, I could almost taste it, milky and sweet. The sight was soft, lightly tinted with pink. It made my eyes relax. I knew it was special, meant to give me a lifetime of calm when I stroked it.

But it was not only the gifts I loved. Just like my father, he felt like a sturdy tent around me. When he hugged me, I felt warm and safe. Partly, I guess, because he was so handsome and big – almost five-and-a-half feet tall. I liked it when he sometimes brought his son Job with him. Not that Job paid any particular attention to me. He was older, by about two years. But Adah and I liked to look at his bronze skin, even darker than mine, just barely hiding his developing muscles. He was tall for his age, and nice too. When he was there, he sometimes made the boys let us play their games.

The visits of the Council of Elders were exciting, but not in the same way as those from unexpected strangers. Plans were made ahead of time for a feast, so there was not so much last-minute rushing around to prepare it. There was not as much curiosity either. Their meetings were important. After all, they did govern all the branches of our tribe spread out over great distances. But there were not many surprises.

Often they met after most of us had moved into town for the winter. I liked being in town, especially when Adah's family and mine occupied the brownish pink caves near each other, cozy escapes from very busy, cold wintry days. When we were living in our tents outside the city, we tended to play mostly outdoor games, when the boys would let us. But when the colder months came, we liked playing inside in the warm dimness. It felt like these rock strong homes had always been there, waiting for us, and always would be. Even the damp, sweet, biting smell gave a feeling of coming home when we settled in. The older and stronger we got, though, the less time we had to play.

Not everyone could spend most of their time in the city. Many of the men had to take turns tending the herds. It was not all play for the rest of us either, because that is when we planted our fields, usually in early winter when the rains made the ground soft enough to plow. Usually we planted outside the town, but sometimes we were able to buy land inside the city walls. My father explained our tribe was good at making the size of our herds bigger, and we were lucky bad weather and bad men had not made much trouble for us, so we had the wealth we needed to buy land.

"Riches buy respect," he explained. "Townsfolk looked down on us as outsiders at first, but later they thought we had more value as people because we had more wealth. No one ever owns land forever, though. Eventually it goes back to the town, usually after such a long time that it will not make a difference in our lifetime."

It was mostly the men who cleared the fields, but we were all involved in planting and weeding. When I was a little girl, my little brothers and I would be there with my mother and father, helping to drop the seeds or even walking alongside one of them as they pulled the plough. It was not an easy job because it was cold and wet, and our soggy clothes hung heavy on our bodies, but it had to be done when the rains came.

Millet, lentils, peas, watermelons, and muskmelons were staples. Wheat made the best bread, but it was more particular about the soil it grew in, so we always planted barley as well because it was willing to grow in poorer conditions. We knew we would have enough to eat when we saw the lush greenish-gold fields of barley emerging in the spring rains. But before those days came, we were all out in the fields, hoeing to keep the ground free of weeds.

The hardest work came in tending the flax, grown for use as lamp wicks and the making of linen fabric. When the flowers appeared, they looked like a rug of aquamarine, so beautiful it almost tasted good, and so different from the colors my mother dyed for her weaving. The fact is, though, the fields were lovely for a reason that also made it hard for us. The flax were grown very close together to keep them growing straight. That meant hard work for our mothers and us children. It was not possible to remove the weeds between the flax in any other way than by squatting down and pulling them out, and that work never ended until harvest time. Then we still all had to bend and squat to pull up the plants when they were ready. They were not easy to gather. They were not easy to turn into linen either, another job for our mothers.

But before we could harvest the flax, the early spring rains came, swelling the grain, a happy sight, and one that meant our work did not stop. First it was the barley, then the flax, which needed a long dry period to be ready for harvest, and then the wheat. During the season of harvest, we were all busy, reaping, threshing and winnowing.

Wherever our mothers went, we went too. That is what mothers did, take care of us while they did their chores. That meant we also worked at whatever we were big and strong enough to do. As for Adah and me, we liked it when we were permitted to be together with her mother or mine. With her, the work felt a little more like play. Some of the women were not in the fields, though, staying behind to wet nurse the babies.

Work never stopped, not even after the grains had been harvested, winnowed, and stored, for the flax had to be prepared for use. Some of the flax seeds that were not left for preparing the next year's crop were stored to make medicine; some were made into oil. The flax itself was soaked, then dried, the outer part used for lamp wicks and the whiter inner part to be made into thread.

Always in the background there was the mixture of rain on the skin and clothes, or swirling heat in the dry seasons, and the sweet odor of growing things.

Adah and I complained sometimes that we were working too much and did not have enough time to play. So did the other children. Most of the time, though, we just went with our parents, like grown-ups, because that is the way things were. Besides, we wanted to be safe with our mothers and fathers.

3

The Coupling

The fear of attack was always in the back of my mind, ever since the time those visitors came and I learned that there were cruel people who might do awful things to us. But as I approached eight years old, something else happened that upset me just as much, maybe even more, because it seemed so personal. It started when our friend Jarna ran to Adah and me one day, screaming in tears. At first she could say not a word, she was sobbing so hard. Her clothes were so wet with her tears that the linen was clinging to her in beer-colored streaks. We were afraid maybe the attackers were coming, but it turned out to be an attack of a different kind. Finally, through her gasping sobs, she was able to choke out a broken portion at a time.

"My father is … betrothing me to an old man … an ugly old man … at least forty-five … all wrinkled and dried up. He … already has three wives … but… they are getting too old … to have babies, so he wants me … I begged my father not to do this … Even my mother did, but … my family needs the bride price … He will pay a lot for me … I have no choice."

It took her a long time to say this, gulping air so hard in-between. But then she could say no more. She just cried and cried as she ran off toward the edge of the camp, the sounds growing more and more like an animal moaning in the distance.

Adah and I sagged our way to a nearby acacia tree to put our dolls to sleep, but even they seemed to droop in our hands. Then it happened like an explosion, I screamed out a big rock from my throat even as Adah sounded like she was about to vomit. Our shaking loosened our tears and we too cried and cried and cried.

This is too terrible. It is as if Jarna is dying.

After a while the unhappy storm calmed into little gasps, and then into sighs that hurt all the way inside, leaving us dry and empty as if something had died in us too. All of us had been looking forward to our betrothals and, as we came closer to the right age, we spent more time imagining what it would be like. But I had never imagined anything so dreadful happening to any of us. I was hurt, sad, scared, and furious. Unfair things made me really angry.

How can her father be so mean? Could Adah's father do such an awful thing? Could my father...? No, of course he would not. Still ...

Adah and I dragged ourselves away from the tree to join our other friends, trying to act like everything was as usual, but I could not calm down inside. I was so upset I slept hardly at all that night. Even holding Astarte was no help, nor was holding my doll. I just could not get the picture out of my mind of poor Jarna living with those old ladies and having to sleep with that ugly old man.

The next morning I felt like a thunderstorm inside. I had to do something, anything. I could not just go on as if this were an ordinary day. What I really wanted to do was pick a fight, but I had no success trying to do that with Adah because she was feeling the same way I did, and all we could do was make each other more upset. We tried all kinds of things; we ran around in circles; we picked up our dolls and put them down; we tried to pick a fight with the boys, but they just ignored us. Of course, that made us even madder. Why should boys be allowed to treat us as if we were so unimportant? Then we would return to the picture of how our poor friend Jarna would suffer.

When I finally returned to our tent, my mother and a couple of my aunts were weaving. I wanted to help them. I thought maybe that would calm the storm. But there was no more room at the loom. Besides, this was a very intricate piece, and my mother probably thought I was not yet skilled enough.

"Dara, get busy carding some wool."

What does she think I am? Some stupid little kid? Maybe my mother and father really do think I am just something to order around.

Jarna's problem seemed to become more and more personal. Maybe something awful could really happen to me too. My whole body burst into anger. The more I thought about poor Jarna, and the danger I might also be in, the more I fed my fury.

What if I tell my mother why I am upset, and she acts like it is nothing at all to worry about? Maybe that would mean that she might treat me the same way.

Finally I got the courage to lean into my mother's lap, forcing my head up between her busy hands.

"Mama, Jarna's father has betrothed her to an old man," I half whispered, my throat squeezing in on itself.

I could not hold my body firm. My eyes picked up every detail of my mother's face. Now I knew I was frightened, and even being frightened scared me.

What if she acts like there is no reason for concern? What would that mean for me?

She already knew about Jarna, and that made me even angrier and more afraid.

She is acting like this is nothing to feel bad about. Astarte protect me.

I wanted to run to Astarte's protecting body, but I could

not move away from my mother. I had to know …

"Why are you not upset? Does it not anger you that her father can just do that to Jarna? Do you not think it unfair?"

My legs, my arms, my whole body grew hard with trying to hold back the trembling when she said, "That is just the way it is, Dara. I do feel very sad for Jarna, but unfair? Her father does have the right. He is the father." My stomach suddenly felt empty and full at the same time.

"But my father would not do anything so mean, would he?" I pushed out my words through teeth holding tight against each other.

My mother's face turned gentle, and I knew her answer. My body yielded its stress and turned away from the pain in my stomach to the questions in my heart and head.

"Why is Jarna's father like that?"

"Jarna's father has a very large family to take care of. And they are so poor that he has a hard time providing them with everything they need. If he is to be able to care for the rest of the family, he must get the bride price Jarna's betrothed has offered."

I could not accept that answer, not with all I had been taught about hospitality and sharing what we had with the rest of the tribe.

"We have enough wealth, why can we not give him some of what we have? Why cannot all our families get together and give him what he needs so he does not have to do that?"

"Because, Dara, that would be an insult to her father. It would be humiliating for him. We would be dishonoring him. We cannot do that to another man in our tribe."

The notion that helping could dishonor and humiliate someone did not make sense to me. I could not accept it. It just was not fair. I was only half listening to my mother's explanation.

"I wish I were a man. They can do whatever they want. Why should his feelings be more important that Jarna's? And what about her mother, just letting it happen? And you? You do not sound at all upset about it."

"Dara, you must learn that the father is the head of the family. He has final control over everyone else. That is just the way it is. As for Jarna's father, he is a good man, and the husband he has chosen for her is a decent and gentle man as well."

I chose to ignore what she said about Jarna's father. I was too busy reacting to the idea that someone else would have final control over me.

"Does it not anger you that you have to just accept whatever your husband may demand?"

I was doing what I was so good at – picking a fight when I was upset.

"But I do not have to just accept what my husband decides to do, because my father was good to me when he chose my husband. Your father respects me – and us."

"I do not believe it. I hear him when he is arguing with you."

"Oh, but Dara, that is the point. We do argue. I know some mothers and fathers who do not argue, but I will tell you right now, the wives do not argue because they do not dare. They have to worry about being divorced and sent away or being displaced by a second wife or a concubine. Your father and I argue because he holds me in high regard. Otherwise he would never listen to what I say, and I would never dare say it."

I had to stop. I did not want to admit that I might be wrong, but I could find no good argument to come back with. My body was feeling softer and more flexible as I realized my mother and I were sitting cross-legged next to each other. She had stopped weaving, paying full attention to our conversation.

She did not stop there.

"You know, Dar', you could help Jarna if you would stop being so indignant and go talk to her. I know this seems awful, but there are some advantages to being one of several wives. If she does not like lying with her husband, she probably will not have to endure it very often. That duty will be shared with the other women. And when she does get with child, she probably will not have to be with him at all. Besides, there is no reason to believe the other wives will be awful. They just might be very kind and helpful to Jarna, like having several mothers who care about her and about her children when she has them. Her life might even be quite easy."

That is hard to believe. But perhaps she is right. She usually does tell me the truth. If he is a good and gentle man, and his other wives are kind and generous, then maybe Jarna will have a large new family to love and care for her.

Obviously that possibility had not occurred to me, but now that the seed had been planted, I could hardly wait to spend time with Jarna, telling her what my mother had said. Maybe it would make her feel better.

I found Jarna sitting under one of the few acacia trees on the outskirts of our camp. Maybe "sitting" isn't the right word. She was humped over under the angled branches as if her body were not even hers but just belonged to whatever she happened to be near. It was hard talking to her because she did not move even as I came closer, so I had to bend and twist to fit under the low branches. The position hurt me, but I think she just felt nothing at all. In fact, I think she did not want to feel or think, or even hear what I was saying, but I kept on talking.

After a while, though, she noticed how uncomfortable we both were and moved away from the center of the tree so we could fit easily in the shade of the outer branches. She still did not say anything, but I think she was beginning to come back to life. I sat with her for a long time, talking, watching her breathe again, and seeing bronze color creep back up her face. By the time we left the tree together, I think she felt much better, maybe just because I stayed with her so long, but also perhaps what my mother had said was helpful.

In the days to follow, Jarna was able to play with us again, though I must say she was not as joyful as she had once been.

As for me, the day came when my mother and father gave me wonderful news. Job! I would be betrothed to Job! Uncle Ruel's son, Job! Someday Uncle Ruel would be another father to me. Job! Job was just the right age too, only two years older than I. Happy thought piled on happy excitement. My body wanted to run out and tell everybody in the camp, but the best I could do was let my legs take turns dancing as I tried to stay still and listen some more.

I knew I loved Uncle Ruel. I suppose I should have realized that he was wealthy, considering the wonderful gifts he brought me when he came. And I should have known he was an important person, given the special way he was greeted when the Council of Elders met here. All I cared about, though, was that I would be related to him even more closely and that I would eventually be Job's wife.

My father did not have to ask me whether it was acceptable to me, but he did. I hardly listened to him as he made an almost formal speech.

"This contract is important because it protects you. Once you are committed to Job, no one else can marry you by force."

I felt that wonderful big tent of comfort surrounding me like when my father, or Uncle Ruel, hugged me. I thought of Jarna, too. At least she is protected from being married by force to someone who might be violent and cruel.

Thank you, Astarte. You have taken care of me more than I could ever imagine.

My mother explained they would plan a celebration in honor of this, but, as I already knew, I would not be marrying Job until I began to bleed. All I wanted now was to hug my mother and father, embrace Astarte, and run out to tell Adah.

I did not even bother to throw my shawl over my head to protect from the weather. The warmth was so high inside me that the raindrops felt like sizzling pellets of summer heat. For me, everything everywhere was bright sun, even as I imagined high temperature waves rising from the ground, stroking me from the feet up. I must have been casting out bright rays from all over my body so even Adah could tell something wonderful was happening to me.

"Job? The nice one we like to watch when he comes? The one whose father is so rich? Job? The handsome one? The tall one? Thick black hair? Beautiful, strong face? Muscles? That Job? The one who lets us play the boys' games? Oh Dar', you are so lucky."

We jumped up and down, both of us laughing, and crying a little too. We went to tell our dolls the good news. Then Adah ran with me to make another visit to Astarte to thank her again for granting me this wonderful thing. I could not stop moving. My heart was pounding too much to stay still. We ran together to find some carob in celebration.

But what about Adah? What will happen to her?

Even as I thought about Adah, she said it. "What will happen to me? Oh please, let us visit Astarte again and ask her to protect me."

It was only a matter of weeks before Adah's father and mother sat her down to hear the speech about betrothal protecting her. Her betrothed would be Narmer. What a relief. Narmer's family always lived close to us, so we knew him. Like Job, he was two years older than we were, and really nice, too. Unlike Job, we saw him all the time, not just when he happened to come to visit.

Adah did take time to cover her head when she came to tell me and she did not send out bright rays the way I had, but she was relieved. So was I. Again we visited Astarte, first fashioning doves from acacia blossoms to present in thanks for her love and kindness.

Narmer's family was not as wealthy or important as Job's, but then, we knew no other family that was. Besides, wealth seemed to be more important to our fathers than it was to us. We did not usually play at being rich, though we did often imagine that we had wonderful jewelry. Of course, we never pretended to be really poor. Until Jarna's experience, I would not have known what that meant. Our tribe in general lived with just enough to eat and protect us from the weather. It is only when we compare ourselves to others who have more that we begin to feel poor.

Adah and I were both happy and relieved with the choices that had been made for us. Now we could enjoy playing wedding, marriage, and family. It was all the more fun knowing who our husbands would be. Now we could picture our own husbands and children around the potage in the evening.

I think my parents had chosen to begin this process in the winter because my father could be around more often and Uncle Ruel would be freer to travel. The crops had been planted, but were not yet ready for hoeing and weeding, committed to future growth, but not yet ripe. A little like me, I guess. And my brothers were in charge of herding the flocks outside the city. Mostly my father just had to show up to supervise. So this was a good time for the betrothal ceremony.

Looking back, that was almost better than our marriage rite. Job and I were the center of attention, and there was feasting and celebration with the whole family, and Adah. Best of all, everything went back to normal when it was done. It was like a wonderful game.

Our betrothal day began when a couple of my married sisters came by early, placing special cheeses and other food near the cooking pot, and then going into the women's quarters with my mother and me and some of our aunts. Not only did they bring special foods, but they came looking special themselves, wearing bleached white linen with their indigo tunics and headscarves. Being older, they had gone through this process themselves, and while they were getting me ready for the ritual, they bubbled with stories of their own betrothals and marriages.

"Remember when Papa called you my name by mistake?"

"Yes," my sister joked. "Just think. Your poor husband might have been stuck with me."

"And what about Mama at my wedding?" giggled the oldest. "She kept forgetting things she was supposed to do."

"Well, after all," my mother defended herself, "it is a big day in a mother's life when her first daughter gets married. It is not easy to send her off to another woman's home. And besides, it meant I was getting old."

"You? Old?" My sisters all gathered around her with hugs.

"Well, she is certainly older than I am, and she always

will be." That was my aunt, my mother's younger sister, joining in the teasing.

I guess in years to come I will also talk and laugh about my betrothal day celebration. Right now, though, I just cannot imagine ever being older or happier than I am today.

My body felt very solidly grown-up, and yet jittery, excited all over.

Except for my wedding day, I would never again have the special kind of attention I had that afternoon. The women helped my mother bathe me in expensive oils, smelling sweet of lilies of the field and Spikenard, and dressed me in a new ankle-length, milky white linen tunic with a blue silk sash and a deep blue robe over it. The feel of the fabric was especially soft since my mother had prepared the thread with particular care, making it possible to weave it into unusually fine linen. It was a grown-up, once-in-my-lifetime outfit.

I have to admit I was in constant excited motion, jiggling from one foot to another, swinging my hips, shaking my hair, and chattering just for the sake of chattering. They had to keep telling me to calm down so they could finish the job. The men outside the women's tent must have felt a little happy themselves, just hearing all the laughter.

When I was all dressed, my long thick black hair was tied back with a silk scarf that matched the sash and they braided in some beads of pink, blue, and violet.

Look at those beads. They are the same color as the beads in my dolls hair. So many years I have been playing grown-up with Adah, and now I almost am.

When I was ready, I was allowed to leave the women's tent with the stern warning not to get dirty.

Of course, the first thing I did was go to Adah's.

"Oh, Dara. You look so beautiful."

41

I knew she was happy for me, but maybe she was wondering whether she would ever look so special. As time for the ceremony drew closer, she seemed quiet. Maybe she was just sick of hearing about Job all the time now. But it seemed like there was something else, almost as if she were angry with me for some reason.

"Are you mad at me, Adah?"

"What a stupid thought. Of course I am not mad at you. You are my best friend. Why would I be angry?"

I was not convinced. There was something wrong. The air had a feeling of a sandstorm brewing, but there was no storm.

I was happy though, that Adah and her family were to be included in the celebration along with our more immediate relatives, and she was happy to be dressed in her good clothes for it. It would not seem right for special things to happen for me without her there.

When Adah and I got back, the rest of my family had begun to gather. It was so beautiful, seeing them all dressed up, creating a swing and flow of blues, yellows, oranges, blinding white, and calming tans.

Then Uncle Ruel rode in, trailed by his whole family: Job, all his brothers and sisters, and his mother. The bright colors their camels wore with regal pride almost outshone the beauty of the women's garments. The sights that I drank in most eagerly, though, were the bejeweled flowing sleeves of the adult women, especially Job's mother's in royal blue, so heavy with precious stones they seemed almost too heavy to move. I knew Auntie Beta. She was nice enough, and I did love the beautiful jewelry she wore, but I liked it better when I had Uncle Ruel all to myself. Things were a little stiff. Uncle Ruel's arrival seemed different from his usual visits – more special. Indeed, it was more special. I circled around him first like he was some sort of strange animal. When I did go to him, his hug felt wonderful as usual. Uncle Ruel laughed his really nice laugh, and pulled me back for another embrace. "This is a very happy day for us, Dar'." And he gave me a special present. It was a gold chain with a figure of Astarte suspended on it. I loved it, and felt especially protected by it. I wore it every day until well into my marriage.

Job was all dressed up too. He was also wearing new linen: a tan loincloth that went down to his knees with a purple tunic over it and a sash of deep brown. Over all that, like me, he was wearing a robe of deep blue. Suddenly I felt very uneasy with him, and he seemed to feel the same way.

Is he content to be betrothed to me? Maybe he does not want to be. Maybe he likes someone else. Maybe his father forced him to do this. Still, he does not look unhappy, just shy. I guess I probably look the same way to him.

Job sent a quick look in my direction. It did not look like the expression of someone who was feeling sorry for himself. I had the feeling that a hug from Job would feel every bit as good as the one from his father, but of course I could not test that out.

When the families were gathered, we got really formal, men in a group in front, and the women behind. Then followed a very proper ceremony in which the fathers signed the betrothal agreement. It included a list of the gifts that would be exchanged when we got married. I guess it was the price my father was paying to get Uncle Ruel to accept me for Job, and my father's reward for giving me away. I was thinking good thoughts about the whole thing. It seemed very good to me that Job and I would eventually be starting off with a large herd of cattle and sheep, and even some donkeys and a camel. I was not unhappy either about the gold I would be receiving.

The ritual went on with my father praising Uncle Ruel as the most desirable man one could want for a father-in-law, and, to hear my father say it, Job was a treasured, extremely valuable, unblemished lamb. Uncle Ruel returned the favor with all kinds of praise for my father. You would think he was the King Almighty. As for me, I might as well have been Astarte for the way Uncle Ruel made me sound like a goddess. I was tempted to believe all the nice things that were being said, especially about me.

The rites ended when my father placed his hands on Job's shoulders, saying, "You will be my son-in-law."

Uncle Ruel did the same to me, saying, "You will be the wife of my son, Job."

I was very happy at the idea of being really related to Uncle Ruel.

And speaking of Astarte, I kissed her frequently on my gold chain during the ceremony and I paid a visit to our household Astarte right after the ceremony, along with my sisters and brothers and Adah. I was so grateful to her. I owed her so much gratitude. Together we brought her a tribute of pomegranates, opened the way she liked it so the beautiful pink seeds showed.

The rest of the day was spent feasting. It was better than when strangers came to stay, because this time Job and I were honored guests, and I did not have to worry whether there would be a share of the roasted sheep for me. Job and I, though, made a wide circle around each other. We just did not know how to act in this new situation. Neither one of us was very relaxed in our special clothes. It was a lovely, cool day, the best of the winter season – no rain, but no high heat lapping at our feet either. The blue of the sky bathed us in comfortable warmth, and our acacia trees seemed greener than ever they had been, tinged with white reflection, a firm outline against the mauve sky.

The next morning we were back almost to normal. Breakfast was a little different because we had some things left over from the celebration of the day before. People had brought dried figs, raisins, and some almond and pistachio nuts from the market. I especially enjoyed the different cheeses my sisters had provided. The leftover bread was special too, made from wheat instead of barley. I tried to make my specialness last longer.

"Mama, can I not enjoy being special for another day? Just for this morning could someone else sweep the tent?"

"The work does not get special, Dara. It does not go away, and neither does the responsibility to do one's share."

My body just would not stay calm enough to bend over and sweep. I needed something larger to do. I guess my mother could tell how I was feeling.

"I can see you are very restless, Dar' Take the food to the people tending the sheep instead. That will give you a chance to run a bit."

Of course I went to find Adah to go with me. She was still acting a little strange, I thought.

"I cannot go with you. My mother has chores for me to do."

"But Adah, we can do what we always do. I will help you with your tasks after you keep me company on mine."

"No, I just cannot do that."

Again I asked Adah if she was mad at me for some reason. She said she was not, but it felt to me like she was. For a long time after that, there was that little feeling that something was different.

4

The Stirring

The events of our betrothals slipped pretty much into the background as Adah and I went on with the process of growing up. It is true that when we played at marriage it could be more real for us, knowing who our husbands would be, and the same thing was true of seeing ourselves as mothers. But we were also occupied with the pleasures of doing things that we could not do when we were really little.

Adah and I loved the grown-up task of going to the market together. I liked that I had authority to pick out the purchases to bring back to my family, usually imported onions and garlic and occasionally fruit and nuts, but also sometimes pretty pottery for food storage, nicer than what we could make ourselves. We could not buy the jewelry and precious oils we loved looking at, but just looking was fun. Sometimes I got to bring some of our woven cloth or hangings to trade. They usually sold right away, because they were very beautiful and, to tell the truth, I was quite skilled at bargaining. I was allowed to use some of the profits to buy some carob beans for Adah and me to enjoy on the way back to camp.

I also enjoyed the job of drawing water from the well, or taking it from the cistern when we were living in town. That was harder work than going to the market, but it was also a grown-up task that made me feel tall and important. I especially liked it when I got to walk home with one of our more beautiful pottery containers on my head.

In truth, life was quite uneventful - until I was about eleven. Then it began to happen. It was not as if I had not seen it begin for the older girls in the tribe, but then I was only watching. This was really personal. I hardly noted what was occurring until one morning, as I was packing some fruit into flat bread for my breakfast, I noticed I was looking almost straight into my mother's eyes. It frightened me almost as much as the sight of strangers riding into the camp had done way back when I was really little.

Something is happening. I am almost as tall as my mother. Am I starting the change?

I drew back into the women's tent so I could feel my body. As I feared and hoped, my hands did not go straight down when I felt my hips, but followed a little curve. Bumps the size of olives were growing on my chest. I ran my hands over my face, pretending to wipe off water that I had just splashed on it, feeling a new hardness in my cheeks, as if a potter had tried to make me look more like Astarte.

I reached back to touch my black hair, even pulling some of it forward so I could look at it. It felt heavier and thicker, more grown-up, somehow. I had never before paid so much attention to my body, which was feeling a little like it didn't belong to me. I really liked that the skin on my arms had a new touch of iron glow in a field of bronze, making it a little more like Adah's. When I stepped back into the main tent, I felt like I had a secret to hide. Nothing looked or felt quite the same. No one seemed to notice that I was no longer Dara. I was someone else. Yes, I knew this would happen, but now it was real, making me feel like a stranger.

Keeping my discovery to myself, I pretended to go on as if everything were the same, but in the days that followed I began to tickle and weaken inside in some ways and strengthen in others, some parts of me getting soft and spongy while my spine felt like it was getting firmer.

I had sometimes played with my hair, tying it up with

jewels, but now it seemed to be much more fun and important, as did rouging my face and lips. Instead of carob, I wanted to buy some of the Salt Sea mud that was supposed to make me more beautiful. It took more effort to do my chores, because I wanted just to sit around and feel these strange sensations. Adah and I also liked being with the other girls at the well where we could compare each other's transformations. Fortunately, Adah was going through changes at the same time I was. Her hair became even springier and her sandy skin darkened a bit. Like me, she grew taller, but not by as much, so we were now seeing each other eye-to-eye.

We knew we were going through the awakening that would lead soon to the flow of blood and then marriage. Excited but scared, we wanted to play mother with our dolls, and we wanted to put them away. We wanted everyone to look at our specialness, and we wanted to hide. Soon we would be joining the other women once a month away from everyone else. I was afraid mine would not flow at the same time theirs did, and I would have to be isolated alone.

My parents probably noticed the things that were happening to me even before I did, though I confess I tried to hide them even as I wanted to show them off. For some strange reason, it was both embarrassing and a source of pride, neither of which I felt like talking about with anyone but Adah. It was scary too, because I realized that soon I would be moving away from my parents and brothers and sisters and I would be a wife and mother belonging to another family a full day's journey away.

Of course, I began to pay more attention to Job when he was around. He was probably paying me more notice too. Maybe because I knew I would become his wife, and maybe because it would have happened anyway, peculiar sensations began to creep in when he was near. Then I would feel a tingle in my belly while the rest of my body went limp. I really wanted just to faint against him and flow into him. He was so handsome with his thick black hair and the pointed beard he was growing. Now he was even taller than he had been when we were betrothed, taller than most of the other boys. I knew I was not allowed, but I wanted to touch him where his muscles glistened and rippled in a very grown-up way. I was coming to love him, I suppose.

The feelings I had for Job were confusing for me, but I wanted to hold them secret to myself. I did not want to admit that I was unsure about anything. My mother was not ignorant, though, and the day came when she sat me down. She did not have to tell me where babies come from. Living in the midst of so many women, and seeing them retreat to the women's tent once a month, and again when they were ready to give birth, had taught me those facts gradually. But I had not expected these feelings inside me, especially the way I felt about Job. It was a relief when she opened up a conversation.

"Dara, come sit by me. Let us talk about your coming marriage. Are you feeling ready for that change in your life? How about Job? Are you happy you will soon be his bride?"

"Oh Mama," I hesitated, not sure I wanted to let her know my secrets. "I feel so funny when I am near him."

"I guess you probably do not know how to talk to him. Maybe it feels strange to know that soon you will be his wife."

"It is more than that." This time I hesitated for a long time before the words erupted. "I really do feel funny. My body feels funny. I get soft inside, and my belly tingles and tickles, almost as if it needs something to eat. And yet it is not like being hungry for food. I am hungry somewhere inside, but not like when it is time for the evening meal.

Oh Mama, I hope you know what I mean, because I do not know how to explain it."

Just trying to describe what my body was doing left me feeling weak.

This is awful. I wish I had not started to tell her. I feel like hot red blood is creeping up from my toes into my head. She must be able to tell that I am having sensations I should not be having. I am afraid she will scold me. But it is like something has exploded inside me, and I cannot stop letting it out.

My mother put her arm around me. It felt warm and good as I leaned into her.

"What you are describing to me is just the way you should be feeling now. You have the body of a growing woman."

She makes me feel so proud, and scared. I do not want to grow up so much that she will stop pulling me close to her like this. But I do not want her to think of me as a little girl anymore either. Maybe I am still just a little girl, and she is telling me these things only to make me feel better.

"But Mama, I see you with Papa, and it does not look like you feel that way with him."

"Oh Dara, I did feel that way about your father when we first married, but love changes over time. I guess you could say at first it is like feasting on figs and pomegranates and special cheeses, and later it is like enjoying the evening potage. The thrill may not be so great later on, but each day it fills the empty hole that would be hunger if you did not have each other."

I liked the idea of being fed in that way, but I was a little disappointed at the thought that this all-body thrill would someday go away. Even though it frightened me, I liked the feelings I had around Job, and I vowed they would never turn to potage. I kept that thought a secret from my mother, though. It would be too much like criticizing her. But she

50

seemed to know what I was thinking. I guess she would be smart about these things after going through it herself, and with my older sisters too, and all the other women of the tribe who raised their tents near ours.

Still, I do think I am different. No one has ever experienced quite these sensations. I will just keep it to myself now, though.

"Dara, I hope you reap great satisfaction from every stage of love. The thrill is something to be treasured, as will be the unbelievable joy of having your first baby together. But eventually the love becomes so much deeper. Your father and I are not separate persons anymore. He and I are fully part of each other."

Yes, that is what I am feeling. I want to be a part of Job — really a part of him.

"I sacrifice daily to Astarte asking that you will feel that same growth of love with Job. You will see. Eventually his happiness will be yours and his pain will be yours. An attack on his body will be an attack on yours and whenever he is spared, you will be spared. And he will know you in the same way."

My mother was a very wise woman.

Once I had discovered the excitement of examining my own body, it became a regular routine as I looked for more changes. Then came the day when I discovered something I knew would change my life forever. The first pinkish-brown stain appeared. I had thought I would be very happy, but I was not. I was confused. Yes, it was exciting to know I would soon be married to Job, but I did not want to leave my mother and father, our local tribe, Adah.

No, Astarte, please let me go back to being the little girl I was.

This time Astarte did not listen to my prayer. She knew it was my time to be a wife and mother. The arrangements that had been made were set in motion.

"Oh Adah. What will it be like? I do not want to be away from you. I want to be married to Job. I want that, but I do not want anything to change. I do not want to leave my family, and what will I do without you every day?"

We sat together in silence for a long time. We had no answer. We wanted to promise each other we would always be together in the same way as now, but we knew that could not be. She would be living with Narmer and I would be with Job. She would bear his children, and I would have many offspring with Job. We would be busy wives and mothers. She would continue to live near her parents, but I would be moving a day's journey away. It would be impossible for us to see each other every day. Not wanting to accept it, we went about doing our chores, including a long walk to the market, trying to pretend that nothing was changing.

The din and color of the market made it almost impossible to think about ourselves at all. Everywhere there were the temporary shelters thrown up to protect the wares spread out on the ground. Even the shelters were of different colors and textures, depending on the materials of which they were made. Some of wool spun from black sheep, some from brown, and some from white. And there were rugs thrown up on acacia branches, cut and fitted to the right size to hold them, some of them almost as beautiful as the things my family made in patterns of bright reds, oranges, blues, and even some yellows. The noise was colorful too, so many voices calling out at once, arguing about the best exchange or urging us to buy. And the smells, the pungent onions, sweet aromatic oils, fresh ripe fruits, and even the rotting smell of products left too long in the heat. The odors were so powerful we could almost see and feel them.

Now we were there with orders from our mothers about what to bring home, but we could imagine the day soon when we would be making the choices for ourselves. We would be in charge. And then, when we started having such thoughts, we would make ourselves forget what was coming and just be little girls again, sent to the market by our mothers. No matter what we did or where we were, it seemed like we were little and grown up all at the same time.

One day we put our dolls to bed and remembered a couple of weeks later that they were still sleeping. Playing with them was no longer so much fun. Maybe real life was becoming more interesting? But I was sad. I even apologized to my doll, promising to pay more attention to her. I did not, though. Instead, I tucked her away in a nice bed of colorful broomcorn and wrapped her in a tiny blue and green blanket my mother had woven for her when I was still little.

"I will get you out later for my daughters to play with," I promised her. Little did I know that her play life would be limited when our adopted God declared her to be an idol.

How wonderful to think of having the prestige and authority of a married woman. How awful to leave my family and Adah behind. How scary to be a member of someone else's family and not my own. How strangely lovely to be with Job all the time. How frighteningly exciting the thought of making love with him. How warm to anticipate the kind of "potage love" for Job that my mother described. How grown up to give orders to my servants and children instead of obeying other people's commands all the time. Did I really want all this?

Job was also busy, gathering the wealth he needed to establish our own home. I imagined he was feeling really manly about that. I supposed it might be a little scary, too.

53

Once he was married, he would be responsible for his own herds, our home, and his family. If Adah and I thought the change would be wonderful and scary, I imagine he would feel the same way about what was happening to him. Being grown up did have its drawbacks.

Usually in our tribe, the bridegroom and his family prepared the new home and brought the bride to it on the wedding day as a kind of surprise. I do not think it was so much a desire to do something special for her as it reflected that the husband was in charge and it was his home. Fortunately, Job had learned some important things from his father, so he included me in the plans as he purchased the site for our tent and erected it.

Because of his family's wealth, Job was able to establish a permanent tent inside the town. To care for his flocks, there would be temporary shelters that could be moved, as was our nomadic tradition, from one place to another as weather and water dictated. These would be occupied sometimes by us, but most often by his servants.

It was part of Job's good fortune, and mine, that he was a member of a wealthy family, a fact that became increasingly obvious as plans proceeded. I was overjoyed that the location he purchased for us nurtured fig and date trees, and our own olive trees. He described for me an altogether beautiful setting. Most of all, I loved knowing the land encompassed several precious acacia trees. Because acacia trees are used for smelting copper ore as well as for building, they are very much in demand, so it was truly a luxury to have our own just to give us pleasure.

Arching from a solid trunk, the branches of the acacia tree rise gradually outward and upward to provide wonderfully cool shade on the hottest days of summer, much better than the protection of our tents, which seem to trap old heat inside. But more than that, their flowing shapes, always firm and solid and constant, still change from season to season as their surroundings bathe them in different colors. A burning pink against the yellow fire of the high heat of summer, they seem to turn a deep orange and rust when summer begins to turn to winter, and sometimes they herald an approaching storm in their mauve and black against a brown sky.

More than that, I believed that acacia trees were blessed with a special kind of spirit. My Astarte's beautiful breasts were carved from the hard wood of the acacia tree, wood which also holds up our tents and provides fire to warm us in the winter. I knew that Astarte in her wisdom had provided the earth with deep suckling breasts for the roots of the acacia trees who could reach deep into the ground to the water far below. That is why they survived so well even in times of drought. I knew Astarte would bless our marriage in the same deep and lasting way.

Once Job had described the setting of our future home, I could hardly wait to see it. Of course, I wanted to share that joy with Adah. It was a full day's distance from my family's location, so it was not an easy project getting there. But my family put together a traveling group to pay a visit to the home of Uncle Ruel and my future mother-in-law, close by Job's property. Two of my sisters, a few of their older children, two of my brothers-in-law, and one of my brothers escorted Adah and me, traveling by donkey, sometimes riding the beasts and sometimes walking beside them.

The journey was almost as exciting as my betrothal ceremony had been and my anticipated wedding would be. On the trip, I was especially aware of the beauty of the land. We passed groves of sycamore trees rising full and thick from their wide bases on the ground, gleaming white in reflected sunlight, with leaves both silver and green protecting the rose red fig. The groves came to life with shepherds who were busy piercing the skin of the fruit so it would ripen. Further on there were clusters of spiny thistle with its pink flowers. At one point we passed a huge, wind-shaped mushroom, its large head standing out against the pink and yellowish tan starkness of the desert around it. Further on I was bathed in nostalgia as we saw in the distance a field of the pink rock rose that had provided the scent of the oil Uncle Ruel had given our dolls many years before. Everything seemed so bright and beautiful as to be unreal. My body swelled and trembled with exhilaration almost beyond containment.

Arriving at Uncle Ruel's long, deep tent, ebony black from the color of the sheep whose hair had provided its fabric and deepened over time by the action of the sun, we were greeted with a celebration of music and food beyond what any of us had anticipated.

As the servants laid out the elaborate feast, musicians appeared with goatskin bags fitted out to provide music. They blew on a short thin bone to swell the bag with air that was then squeezed in and out while a tone was created by fingering the holes in a longer bone on the other side of the instrument. Their heavy tones supported the lightness of the flutes and harps, while the clapping together of elaborately carved ivory sticks spelled out an irresistible rhythm.

The joyful surprise swelled into swirls of dancing and laughter. As I twirled around and around in the dancing circle, my ecstatic pleasure was tempered only by the thought that things could not possibly get any better – that my wedding day might seem less by comparison.

In the midst of the merriment, I felt a jagged edge of

excitement travel up my arm. It was Job touching me to lead me off, followed by several singing and dancing small groups accompanied by the musicians, to the location of my future home with him.

It was even more lovely than I had anticipated, the trees and surrounding fields of wild flowers seeming magical. Oh, how thankful I was for Astarte's blessing! Job tried to draw our future tent for me in my imagination, but I was too taken with the location to even want to bother imagining more.

There was room for most of our party to sojourn in Uncle Ruel's ample tent that night, but his servants had also raised another one on his property for some of the men to stay. The welcome could not have been any more wonderful. Equally grand was the morning feast he provided before seeing us off to return home the next day.

We hadn't been on our way very long, however, when I felt my attention drawn away from the beauty of all that I had seen and enjoyed on this journey.

My chest is feeling so tight. It is so hard to breath, like a sandstorm is on its way. Oh, Astarte, guide us to the safety of home before it attacks us.

I looked around me, expecting to see everyone gathering speed to get to safety before the storm came. Strangely, they were all still laughing and making music as if nothing troublesome were happening.

It is so hard to breathe. The atmosphere is pressing against my chest. I do not want to die now. Everything has been so beautiful. To be exposed to a sandstorm would be a terrible thing. All my dreams of marriage and joy may not come true. I cannot seem to breathe in enough air. Why is everyone else ignoring the signs?

Only Adah was subdued. I kept my fears to myself,

confused as I listened to the singing and laughter of my companions. My body focused on stretching my chest to take in enough air. I just wanted to get home safe.

Strangely, even when I mentioned the weather change after we arrived home, no one else admitted having experienced it. Only Adah seemed to feel it.

My family began preparing my wedding clothes. Job's family was doing that for him, too, because for our wedding we would be really dressed up, king and queen for a week, you might say.

Now it was time for Job's father to pay my father the dowry they had agreed on. Partly that was to make up for the fact I would no longer be around to work for the family, but it was a kind of protection for me too. Even though my father could use it, the assumption was that some of it would be available for me in case I should become widowed or divorced.

It was also time for my father to give me the gifts he had agreed on. Part of that dowry consisted of gold coins that were made into a circlet for my marriage headpiece.

All in all, it was expensive for my family. I began to realize why Job and I would want sons rather than daughters who would cost a lot and eventually leave the family. Even though dowries might be expensive, sons would remain in the family to continue working. And the children Job and I would have would be part of his family's heritage, not mine. That did not mean my parents had no love for the children my sisters already had, and would not love the ones I would birth. But the fact is daughters are of less value in terms of wealth.

As we moved toward our wedding day, I felt less and less like a child. My time with Adah was spent differently, both of us talking about family and children and responsibility

– not playing at it, but planning for it.

"You will see, Adah, things will not be very different for us. My home will still be your second home, just as it has always been, and your home will still be mine."

Adah made no response.

If my betrothal day had been special, it was nothing compared to the emotions the wedding preparations were evoking in me. I began to feel like royalty about to be crowned queen. I had seen my sisters and other young women in our settlement travel this route to marriage, but this time the focus was on me.

I admit I felt really important – and nervous! I was afraid of our wedding night. Suddenly the anticipation of lovemaking was not some kind of vague dream, but a challenge - to enjoy it? To do it right?

Playing at pregnancy and childbirth was giving way to fears that I would not have the traditional strength of the women in my family. I could die giving birth. I could be barren. Would Job stay with me then? Would he divorce me? Would he turn his love and attention to other wives? To concubines? Would I ever come to know the "potage love" my mother described? The anxiety did not terminate my excitement but it was an ever-flowing, contaminating undercurrent.

As for the fear of my wedding night, my three married sisters were of very little help. One sister was almost poetic about how great it would be. Another tried to cheer me up by telling me it would not be so bad after the first lovemaking. A third just complained that the other two should let me find out for myself.

I was not concerned about being happy with Job. I did fear that I might do something to spoil things, but I was confident that Job would be the ideal husband. Sometimes

I did wonder though, if he knew enough about lovemaking to get past my total ignorance.

5

The Consummation

So the activities of the preparation year went on. Job was busy, with the help of his family, preparing our marriage tent. It would be a traditional tent, made of goats' hair fabric held up by stakes of acacia wood, but, because it was erected for permanence, it could have several rooms. There would be a central section generally open on one side, but with a flap that could be closed to protect from sand and wind storms, as well as an occasional driving rain. That was an anteroom where most of daily life would go on: cooking, entertaining guests.

In the beginning there would be two more sections, each set off from the main living area by hangings, which would be beautifully bright and colorful, mostly the creative work of my family. Some hangings, however, would be purchased from passing merchants, like the rugs for the floors.

One room would be for women only. Job would be the only man allowed to enter there. The other room would be sleeping quarters, initially for Job and me, but also for the children who would come, and sometimes for guests. Someday there would be outlying tents for the servants and slaves, but Job was not yet able to acquire such help. We would get to share with his parents, however, a fact that would alter my life more than I anticipated.

There was an urgent necessity to get the basic tent constructed before the rains of early winter came, because until the goat's hair got wet, it would leak. Once it rained, the fabric would close up and it would be waterproof. Only after that could household items be kept inside and dry.

Even as our future home became firm, my hips presented a larger curve to my touch, while my olive size buds grew into something more akin to halved plums. The commitment had been made and the time for our wedding approached. From now on, it was all tradition and ritual that swept us along as if it had a will of its own. Scared and awed as we might be, there was never any thought of turning back.

The air shuddered with anticipation as my family acquired cooking and storage pots and busily wove blankets and additional decorative hangings for my home.

My mother tore into strips the garments I had worn for my betrothal celebration, too small for me to wear now, bleached them in the sun, re-dyed them, and wove a deep blue and green blanket to cover Job and me in our marital tent. When I saw it, I did briefly remember my doll, wrapped in her own blue and green blanket, but my thoughts quickly laid her aside.

More wonderful than any doll was the lovely Astarte my mother had attained to bless my home. Created differently from the Astarte I would be leaving behind at my mother's home, her reddish yellow ample breasts and full hips were formed of pottery clay. Her presence would guarantee my success at birthing many children for Job.

At the time, my attention was completely on Job and me and our coming marriage, so I did not really appreciate that this wedding of mine was a triumph for my entire clan. My father had negotiated a very successful union in joining me to Uncle Ruel's family. As a consequence, my extended family, always traditionally involved in marriage preparations, worked even more diligently and excitedly to prepare for my wedding.

Extraordinary attention was paid to the preparation of

my bridal garments, dazzling in their vivid, joyful colors. The linen undergarment was, of course, particularly soft to the touch, having been carefully prepared by the loving hands of my truly skilled mother. To the eye, it was a thrust of brilliant yellow. When the gaze traveled to the arms, however, even that color paled against the brilliance of the full sleeves, beaded in translucent carnelian of blood-red, orange, peach, and pomegranate rose, along with agate combinations of black, brown, and milky white, and occasional bronze and gold.

It was not only the beading that made the sleeves of such great consequence, but just the fact of full sleeves themselves. They were a mark of wealth, for only women tended by slaves and servants could wear them. They would just get in the way of ordinary nomads doing their daily work.

The sleeves were a temporary tribute to Job and me as to any bride and groom who live for a week like true royalty. Nor would the jewels remain in my possession after the time of wedding celebration. Most were borrowed, supplementing the few that were owned by my family.

For us nomadic women, our marriage feast would be the only time we would expect to wear long, full sleeves. Just like the wedding, it was a special symbol to be enjoyed only once. The sleeves would be removed and the jewels returned to their various owners. I could plan, however, to keep the soft, bright yellow undergarment, without the sleeves, for special occasions.

There is more to describe, a task which helps me keep alive the memory of that time when I felt more vital and significant than ever before or since. Sometimes, when everything turns gray, I am revived by the memory of the splendor of those colors and those days.

Now I know it was not so much the shades and tints of

the events themselves, but the pigments with which my eyes dyed them. How fortunate it was to live those days without seeing what was to come.

And so to continue the description of my glorious wedding attire. Over the bright yellow undergarment was a slightly shorter deep red tunic, and around my waist was a bronze orange girdle, a kind of wide belt also adorned with precious stones. Even my sandals were jeweled.

My veil, dyed and woven by my mother in a blue so deep it was almost purple, rivaled any that the wealthiest of women might wear. Circled by the crown of gold from my father, it would cover my face at the beginning of the ceremony. It is not that Job did not know what I looked like, of course, but it was tradition for me to be presented covered at our bridal ceremony.

Probably because my family was so skilled in the use of color, my eldest sister had become especially talented at creating designs with henna. She made me a gift of that art on both my hands and my feet. Although black when she applied it, over a short time the henna turned to a vibrant bronze.

Never again would anyone spend so much time touching my hands and my feet. She spent a whole day, not long before my wedding, applying the henna so it would be just the right color and last through the early days of my marriage. On my feet and ankles, she applied a lovely intricate pattern. But more exciting to me was what she gave my hands. On the palms, in the center of a lavish design, she sketched a pomegranate, one of the sacrifices Astarte was most pleased to receive. And on the back of my hands was another of my dear goddess's favorites, a sheep.

I was overjoyed to know that my hands, touching Job, would be offering devotion to Astarte at the same time. It helped to reduce somewhat my fears of the wedding night.

And so came the day of our wedding. After a full bath, one of the few I could expect to have in my lifetime, I was covered with precious oils bought especially for the occasion. My long black hair was bound and covered by my jeweled veil, thrown back from my face until time for the marriage rites. My face was rouged and my eyes darkened.

Needless to say, I had never felt so special, with all the women in my family bustling about to make me gorgeous, nor did I expect ever again to feel so well attended.

Job, at the temporary quarters where he and his retinue sojourned outside the area of our camp, was receiving the same care, even being adorned in precious jewels as well.

Knowing the attention he was receiving, I should have expected it, but he still caused me to gasp with joy when he and his family arrived at our tent early that morning. His whole family looked splendid, as did mine. His eldest brother, serving as the "friend of the bridegroom," was magnificent. Looking at him and at his father, Uncle Ruel, I knew I could expect my Job to retain his handsome appearance for many years.

I was reminded of the caution with which Job and I approached and at the same time avoided each other on the day of our betrothal. Again, I felt some of the same strangeness, but it was tinged with a different kind of comfort in knowing that we would be riding side by side to our own home after this ritual. There would be a different newness to overcome, and a new joy in accomplishing it.

A very formal affair followed. I was accompanied by my two beautifully dressed "companions," Adah on one side and my eldest sister on the other. Job and his brother stood apart, waiting for me to be led to them. After the exchange of the gifts that had been promised at the time of our betrothal, my father led me to Job, removing my veil and putting it on Job's shoulder, saying, "The government is on your shoulders."

I wonder how it felt to my father when he did that, basically giving me away. I know I was close to crying, not only from joy.

Then Uncle Ruel said to me, "May you be blessed with a full and happy life and many healthy children."

Adah was given the honor of placing on my head our tribe's bright beaded wedding crown as a sign that I was now a married woman. A stunning piece, weighted by precious stones and with bejeweled bands hanging down around the head and face, it would be mine to wear for the week of our wedding celebration. I know Adah was looking at it with joyful anticipation, aware that soon she would be happily wearing it after her marriage to Narmer.

I confess I was paying very little attention to the larger group that surrounded us, so I was a bit startled when Eliphaz, Uncle Ruel's elderly relative, stepped forward.

"It is my pleasure to represent the hope of the entire clan that your marriage will be fruitful and long lasting."

Then he presented me with a beaded gold necklace.

"This gold represents the protection of your entire family, to be yours in times of joy and times of sorrow, in times of hope and in times of fear, always to belong to you alone so that you may never be poor."

Then he embraced me, kissing me first on one cheek and then on the other.

It was rather stiffly formal. When I saw how people had stepped aside to make ample room for his passage, I realized that he was a very important man, due a great deal of respect as a wise elder. I was honored that such a personage had traveled the long distance from his own country to be here, but I think I felt less awe than the others, probably because I was too busy paying attention to Job.

Following this ceremony, we enjoyed some refreshment: fruit, cheese, wheat bread, and some beer. It was necessary to give us sustenance for the journey ahead. But the real feast and celebration awaited our arrival at our new home, a day's journey away, a journey that began when Job and I mounted the camels provided by his father and mine.

If Job and I were feeling like royalty, I wanted to imagine that our camels did, too. Their colorful protective blankets rivaled anything that had ridden into our camp in the past. In fact, taking in the entire group traveling with us, there was every color and jewel one might imagine, even the purple worn by Job's mother, betoking her honored position.

When my camel knelt low enough for my father to help me board him, it was almost as if he were praying. I wanted to believe he was pleading with Astarte to protect our journey. I certainly was offering that plea.

Oh, of course I know he was just doing what he had been trained to do, but it was very hard on that day not to feel like everything in the world had been put there just for Job and me. We certainly did tower above most of those traveling with us.

Once the entire party was gathered, we proceeded toward our new home. As many people as possible traveled with us in celebration. Not all could afford to be away from their flocks and fields. For those we left behind, there was enough food and beer to provide a feast when they returned.

On the entire journey we were accompanied by music and singing, even more joyful than we had experienced on the earlier visit to Uncle Ruel's. As we approached our home, I dismounted and joined the dancing. So many times my body had been restless with fear or anticipation. This time, my body swayed in harmony with my joy, spiritedly in a rhythmic beat of heart and mind as one, so much in unity that I truly thought not at all about what I was doing as the spirit carried me along.

Fortunately, the heat was not the intense golden waves of summer, undulating ceaselessly and feverishly toward the sky. It was more constant now, almost relaxed as the first part of winter celebrated the planting of the crops and the calmer time of waiting. Warm, carefree, eager, and full, we approached our new life together.

Once we arrived in the area where Uncle Ruel and Job occupied so much of the land, I began to feel the surging waves of heat that were not there on our journey. No one else was aware of them, except perhaps Job. They were raging inside me, interfering with my appetite for all the glorious foods being offered by Uncle Ruel's servants.

To be fair, there was one other person who seemed to know the turmoil that was going on in my belly. Aunt Beta, who was now my mother-in-law, served me a goblet of grape juice even as she laid her hand on my shoulder. Never one to talk much, she spoke kindness and comfort with her gesture. I found myself giving in to the message that we would live well together, now that I was to be her daughter, perhaps more than my own mother's, given the distance we would be living from my old home.

My body joined the feast. And what a banquet it was! So much more lavish than even the most wonderful traditional celebratory meals we nomads were usually able to bring together. The music trembled in my face and ears, and the dancing was a pulsation so complete I had no thought of what I was doing.

Every once in a while Adah and I found each other to exchange excited hugs. Even Jarna was there, shyly enfolding me. In fact, it seemed that everyone was embracing me, and Job. I was happily lost in the ecstasy of this time and place toward which we had all been working for a year.

Then time vanished. Darkness began to close in, and I suddenly felt a powerful urge to seek out Adah, embracing her with a river of tears in which she joined, surprising both of us. No words were necessary. We knew then we would never have the same relationship again. Something vital to both of us was over, though I knew we would be deep friends forever, even though apart. Still, there was grief in this moment of parting.

At that point, Job came up behind me and nudged me gently on the elbow. Sharp bolts of fear, regret, and anticipation burst inside me. I did not want to leave Adah, nor end the merriment. I envied all those with us who were free to go on with the feast. I wanted to go with Job. I did not want to go with Job.

I cannot apply a label to what I was feeling. I did know the goal had been reached and I missed the striving. Now there was a new purpose.

Job guided me into our private quarters. I saw the lovely deep bed of straw, covered by the bleached white bedclothes we would have to stain to prove my virginity. The private feast laid out for us in one section did nothing to relieve the panic that seized me. I had thought Job and I were the center of attention during this whole time of preparation and celebration. Now I knew it had been nothing but a distraction to prevent my thinking of what was about to happen. Job and I were left alone to be the focus of each other's lives.

My dread was worse than anything I had ever experienced in anticipation of the possibility of enemies raiding our camp. And it was different, made worse by some kind of hopeful excitement about what we were doing alone together in this place. I wanted to turn around and run back out to the celebration that was still going on. I envied friends and family out there who did not have to experience what I was going through.

Job stood behind me, knowing, I guess, something of what I was feeling. Maybe he was feeling it too. He whispered, "Do not be afraid." He touched my shoulder, evoking a spark that blazed straight down to my toes.

Then he removed the crown from my head, replacing the weight of it with a throbbing circlet of elation that swirled around my brow and spiraled down through the most private parts of my body. It was almost intolerably breathtaking when he released my hair from the beads that contained it, and fingered it as it fell.

Engulfed by an eddy of unimagined, wonderfully frightening sensations, I turned around to see Job, as if expecting some kind of stabilizing comfort. There, for the first time, facing each other fully, we were joined. He was my husband. I reached out to uncover those glistening muscles I had yearned to touch so long ago. Fear was gone.

I know we folded our elegant garments carefully and put them aside, but I cannot fully recount the route of our early figs and pomegranates and special cheeses love, culminating in the deep yet ecstatic agony as his body filled mine. I think I cried out in pain. I think we laughed some.

The dancing and music continued long into the night and even into the next day. I felt no envy for those outside our tent. No love, I was sure, had ever been as intense as ours. And it was sealed as I finally drifted off to sleep, Job's words giving my body a final caress.

"I am glad our fathers arranged our marriage."

The next morning we woke up together in our private

room in our own tent. One of my first thoughts was of my sister who complained that the other two should let me find out for myself what my first night with Job would be like. She was right. Unlike the preparations that went into making us ready for our wedding, only Job and I could create our marriage.

I felt relieved, deeply happy and very grown up, but also, strangely, a little sad. I had never before been alone with just one person. It struck me that our life would be like this for a while, at least until we had children. On the other hand, I had never been joined with anyone the way Job and I now were.

We were really married, and we had the bloody bedclothes to show for it. It was time to dress again in our ceremonial clothes and present the evidence to my mother, who proudly, with the help of the whole family, paraded it before the crowd.

So, the hard - and wonderful - part had been done. I had expected we could now give the weeklong celebration our complete attention, but it did not happen that way. Our first night together had wrapped us in ourselves and each other in a way that tended to block out concern for what was going on around us.

I felt a kind of power I had never felt before, a kind of solidity from head to toe, yet bold at the same time. There were many times when I would have been happy to leave the crowd to return to our section of the tent with Job. And my attention focused often on the new sensations where Job had broken into my body. Truthfully, I was experiencing pain, but it felt to me like a secret tribute.

I wondered if people could read all these feelings on my face.

Then it was all over, suddenly, even shockingly. The party

ended, the celebrants returned to their homes, and I was part of a new family and a new way of life.

The depth of loneliness was far greater than I had anticipated. Not only did I miss my own family, and Adah, and the others who traveled with us, I missed the very duties that had been the essence of my daily life. Uncle Ruel and my mother-in-law were surrounded by servants and slaves who performed the daily chores. I was not needed to mill the grain, make the bread, sweep the floors, prepare the evening potage, carry food to those tending the flocks, tease the wool, separate the layers of flax, pull the weeds, or even to help plant the seeds.

I realized that my mother had known how great the difference would be when she provided my home with the basic necessities for dyeing and weaving. Spinning was an occupation that I could pursue as well.

Aunt Beta, in her quiet way, also understood. I imagine her life was quite different from the nomadic existence she and Uncle Ruel had experienced when they were first married. For her, the change probably occurred gradually, not so abruptly as it did for me, so she had a chance to adapt to it a little at a time.

At any rate, she did her best to introduce me into my new way of life and to the important, though different, functions I would perform. The very first morning, after Job had gone out to supervise the care of his flocks, she invited me to ride out with her.

"Come with me, Dara. We will visit the tents of those who serve our family."

I recognized that this was the first day of my training in how to be Job's wife. How different it would be from what I had witnessed in my own home. I was afraid.

How can I possibly meet Aunt Beta's expectations? I do not belong here.

She must have read my mind.

"Dara, you will find this strange at first, but all you have to do is listen, remember what is said, and do what has to be done."

Each place we stopped, it was clear people were happy to see her. Mostly we found women caring for small children, running happily about, mostly unclothed, copying, and thereby learning, their mothers' chores. I admired the gentle way in which my mother-in-law took the children into her arms. My body tightened with fear that I could never do as she did even as my heart raced with hope that I might.

At each stop, she inquired about the needs of the people we saw, clearly making mental note of the requests. At some stops, she delivered items such as water jars, rugs, bed coverings, and even some clothing. Some of what she left with the recipients would be used for bartering. Others would be more directly useful. I could see they were all responses to past requests that she found appropriate.

I have not appreciated Aunt Beta's power. Just because she is so quiet in Uncle Ruel's presence, I haven't noticed much about her except her jewelry. I was wrong. She has set me quite a challenge. I pray Astarte will help me do as she does.

My fears eased somewhat as I learned that the cloth she provided was the product of her own hand.

This is good. I can certainly do as well as she does in the task of weaving.

I felt a sense of personal pride and accomplishment knowing I had the skill to make beautiful fabrics. Feeling a bit better about my own ability to carry out the obligations of being Job's wife, I was able to follow my mother-in-law with less apprehension.

I confess, though, that my thoughts were constantly with

Job, enduring frequent stabs of longing for him. I could hardly wait to unite with him over the evening meal we shared at his parent's lavish tent. Even more, I wanted the day to end so I could be alone with him in our own home. My mother's description of a figs and pomegranates and special cheeses love hardly did justice to my feelings for my husband.

Still, I had not anticipated longing so much for my own people, a pang that struck me every evening at mealtime. I even missed the barley bread, rarely provided by Job's parents who could afford wheat on a regular basis. I missed the conversation, and I missed the V of my father's legs as he squatted to hold me. I missed being a child even as I took joy in being a married woman.

I had been in my new home about a week when my mother-in-law ordered a sheep to be sacrificed to my Astarte. It was always Aunt Beta's function to order the slaughter of animals when appropriate, but this sacrifice I recognized was a special tribute to me. I think she recognized my longing for my old home, and perhaps even feared I might lose my dedication to her son. She need not have worried about the latter possibility. Nonetheless, I was touched at the special homage to my goddess.

Loneliness and unease dwindled some with time, and I settled into a kind of routine, enjoying the company of the women of Job's family. The sense of being alone in a new world often attacked me when I was weaving, a task which was becoming a major function and source of pride for me. I wanted to be with my own very talented family then.

The truth is, marriage did change my life in ways that struck me to the core. I was still constantly busy on a daily basis, but with tasks that were new to me. Gradually, my mother-in-law taught me the skill of assessing the value of land that might potentially be purchased as well as flocks that might be added to Uncle Ruel's wealth. What I was learning would add to my value as Job's wife.

Always in the back of my mind during the early months of my marriage, or maybe more often in the forefront, was the expectation that I would soon be with child. Then, I believed, I would feel that I was really becoming useful as a wife to Job and as a member of his family. I even thought I would feel more accepted by all of them as one who truly belonged.

Strangely, when finally I was pregnant, I failed to recognize it right away. I knew I could expect my monthly bleeding to stop when I was pregnant, and I certainly knew that my body would eventually swell with the fullness of the child inside, but I had not expected the subtle feelings I had in the beginning.

Some of it I cannot even describe, but I do know my breasts, now the size of small melons, began to harden a bit, and I was surprised when Job's touch caused them pain. My legs felt more burdened, which made no sense to me because in the beginning they bore no more weight than usual. And my pelvis felt strange, as if someone had inserted a tiny pebble that weighed on me.

At first I thought it was just more of the effects of my frequent lovemaking with Job. Thanks to being with the women, though, I felt free to talk about my feelings, and they were quick to rejoice that I was with child. After all, childbearing is a primary and desirable function for wives. I think one or two of the older women knew just by looking at me, even in the early weeks. I was finally convinced when I felt a little sick in the mornings, though I must say that part was not very bothersome for me.

I was happy. Now I was really a fully mature woman,

worthy of all the respect that goes with it. Well, almost. I still needed the final seal of actually giving birth.

Marriage had taken me out of childhood, pregnancy had taken me well along the road, but the final confirmation of my full value as a woman would be when I actually gave birth to a healthy baby. Of course, I would feel especially wonderful if I gave birth to a boy.

I confess, though, that I also felt fear – fear that I might fail at giving birth, that I might birth the baby too soon, before it could survive out in the world. Or that I might give birth to an unhealthy child.

I did not allow myself to be aware of it often, but I was also afraid I might die. I tried, but could not stop myself from rehearsing the reasons to be anxious, even terrified. There were women in our tribe who died in childbirth, and there were babies born dead.

All the mothers around me understood that experience of frightened joy and, of course, Job's family, like my own, had developed many practices to help assure success and keep me focused on the hope.

I guess the most important thing they did for me was what they did not do. They did not treat my pregnancy like it was some kind of special event. They just took it for granted that I would be successful, and with that kind of confidence around me, it was easier to be calm.

Astarte was a great comfort to me too. I felt that my prayers would be answered by her protection, especially because Aunt Beta was constant in her offerings of sacrifice to Astarte.

Part of the reassurance was found in our rules about how to be pregnant, especially the traditions about food. That made sense because obviously the developing child would be sharing my food to help it grow. At the same time, it needed to be spared foods that might cause it a problem. I was specifically warned to avoid salt and fat, both of which were felt to be dangerous for the baby. Even depriving myself of those foods swelled my sense of pride in what was going on in my womb. Like my betrothal, and later my marriage, I knew I was not the first or only one to have the experience. But this was happening to me, and that was very different from observing it in others.

Otherwise, and surprisingly, life went on as usual while I grew larger and heavier. When I say heavy, I mean specifically that sensation of the little pebble becoming a rock dragging down inside me as the pregnancy progressed.

No one had told me either that I would wake in the night with terrible cramps in my legs, or that my baby would heartlessly and almost constantly beat on me as if angry for being restrained in its inner prison. All in all, when it finally came time to deliver my baby, I was more than ready.

It was time for Job's first child to enter the world.

6

Fruitful And Multiplying

I was almost fourteen years old when the pains began.

I guess there is no better time to be surrounded by a tent full of women than when the agony starts. And I do mean agony. I had heard other women screaming, but did not imagine the intensity of the suffering until I experienced it for myself.

They tell me I did some shrieking too, and I guess that helped to ease some of the tension inside, but I honestly do not remember that. Probably I was too busy hurting to hear what I was doing.

The interesting thing is that now I can talk about the birthing, but I cannot really remember the full depth of it. I guess if it had stayed with me, in all its suffering, I would have been more than terrified when I went through my other pregnancies.

Knowing that I was about ready, we had made some preparations in the women's section of our tent. We had already piled up some large stones, covered by rugs for comfort, for my hips to rest on when pushing the baby out. The rugs were firm, soft, and new, created by my mother and aunts specifically for the birthing of my first child.

They had chosen the soothing colors of green and blue, with a bit of yellow and orange mixed in to reflect the excitement and change surrounding the event.

Offerings had been made to Astarte to help facilitate a healthy delivery, and strips of clean linen had been set aside, along with the aromatic oil purchased just for this birth. I had chosen the aroma of the pink rock rose, the gift Uncle

Ruel had given Adah and me many years ago for our dolls. I loved the scent, but I think also it was a way of bringing my childhood with me to this final move into adulthood.

With all the preparation, and with a lifetime of living with women, I was not surprised by what came next, but I certainly was not fully prepared. Once again there was the truth that this time I was not just watching. It was happening to me.

My mother had begun the journey to my home as soon as she received the word from one of Uncle Ruel's servants that I was about to give birth. I was greatly relieved when she joined my mother-in-law, Aunt Beta, inside the tent. She brought with her a wave of relief and a sense of safety. She also brought pomegranates to offer in sacrifice to Astarte who was watching over the whole process from a corner of the tent.

My mothers kept me walking around, even though I begged to lie down, while the heat seemed to be roaring into the tent from outside and straight to my body. As my married sisters and sisters-in-law joined us, they took on the task of bathing my face and even my body in cool water and oils.

I do not want to make too much of it, but I certainly did enjoy the pauses when the cramping pain let up on its seizing. On the other hand, when the pangs started coming closer together, I was relieved, and so were the women around me, I think.

Finally, it was time. I believe we nomads had an advantage in that we spent so much of our time sitting cross-legged on the ground, or squatting, so we did have very strong legs. And that certainly helped when I was digging my feet deep into the ground as I alternately pushed and relaxed the baby's way out.

The pillars of stone we had constructed supported my hips on both sides, leaving space for the baby to emerge. My mother stood behind me, basically leaning her own body against my back. The other women in the room took turns massaging the area where the baby would emerge, and my mother-in-law stood ready to receive her grandchild when it was born.

Then, as I felt the most intense, tight, painful cramping around my lower abdomen, the women in the room began to get excited, urging me to push. I just wanted to die, but I did press down, almost unthinkingly obeying their instructions.

And then it happened. My first son was born. What happy sounds of celebration and relief came from the women's tent.

I suppose it must have been hard for Job outside with the other men waiting to get the word, but I imagine he was relieved that the sounds were happy.

The baby could not be presented to him until the women had washed him with water, bathed him in the special oil, and wrapped him tight in the strips of linen cloth to help him grow firm and straight. Then Job's mother had the honor of bringing the baby out to him with the announcement, "This is your son."

The men cheered as Job raised his firstborn high in the air and gave him his name. "He will be known as Primus, Son of Job." After he and the men around him had welcomed our boy into the world, Job held Primus close to his breast for a brief period until his mother gently opened her son's arms to release his hold and returned my baby back into the tent.

In the meantime, I had been through the birthing process again. This time it was not so painful, but surprising to me. I had not really understood about the afterbirth, when all that part inside me that had cradled my baby was now expelled.

What pain? Already I could hardly remember what I had just endured. My eldest sister placed the baby to my breast and he began to suck the liquid that came before anything that really looked like milk.

Now the sensations were different. First of all, I felt so light and unburdened. Most of all, I knew the wonderful tickle-tingle in my breasts and my pelvis as the baby drew the life-giving fluid from my nipples. How he did suck! It seemed that he would follow the tradition of Job's family and mine, being a very healthy child.

When all was complete, and I was cleaned, I lay down on the bed of rugs and blankets the women had prepared for me. I would rest for a while as my breasts filled with hearty milk for my son. If I did not have enough for him, he would be brought to a wet nurse. I did not want that to happen, so I rested, and ate the good foods my sisters brought to me, even those prepared with the fat and salt of which I had been deprived while I was pregnant.

Once little Primus had settled into a calm sleep, Job was allowed to come in. He was so happy he even said so. And what a carefully warm and loving hug he gave me. We definitely had not yet reached the "potage" stage of our love. On the other hand, I really wanted no thought of his getting close to me with anything more than his warm embrace. It is a good thing tradition required a long period before we could share a bed again.

I knew some women worried their husbands would go to a concubine during this period, but I had no fear of that with Job. I knew he was faithful to me. Even more important, he was so wrapped up in joy and pride over his son that it was hard for him to think of anything else. Just as I was now feeling like a complete woman, I knew he was feeling whole as a man. My mother was right. There was an amazing shared intimate joy in the birth of our first child. Job and I had become flesh of each other's flesh through marriage. Now that oneness was sealed with this little sleeping fusion of ourselves.

Only one thing was needed to make this day complete, and I asked Job about it.

"When is my friend Adah coming?"

One of my first thoughts when the pain began to seize me had been to ask someone to fetch Adah. Given the distance between us, we saw very little of each other since we both married.

"My sister Tiva traveled with some of my father's servants to fetch her."

I was so grateful to Tiva, and so anxious to see Adah. The truth is, her very presence would make everything seem complete. My love for Job was intense and all encompassing, but it was different from the deep devotion Adah and I had developed in all the years of growing together.

Shortly after I had drifted into a comfortable sleep, I was awakened by an increased intensity of the sounds of people outside our tent. The voices had become louder and more high-pitched as they welcomed Tiva back, escorting Adah.

I think many of the family and their servants were happy for me, pleased to think that I was being given this gift of a visit from my old friend. Now my birthing was complete. Adah was here to celebrate the reality of what had been play for us for so many years.

The months apart had made some changes. Adah was still attired in the off white and brown of our daily nomadic costume, but her face was changed, mostly because there was added bulk in her cheeks. Her eyes even looked different – tired, and yet more brilliantly alive. I realized with joy as my gaze moved on down to her belly that it was full. I wondered if my face and eyes had displayed such changes when I was growing Primus inside me.

Adah's presence bathed me in a sense of comfortable completeness. After all, had our lives not been built on the anticipation of these moments of birth? Knowing that she was about to join me in motherhood brought our friendship full circle. I was contented for myself and our relationship and very happy for her.

We exchanged a long, tight embrace, and I asked, "How long will it be before you give birth?"

"Another month, Dara, so I guess once again you have moved ahead of me."

Then, of course, she wanted all the details of my birthing process, shared intimately and comfortably with her as I could do with no other.

Adah sojourned with us for a night, staying with me in the women's section of the tent. It was easy for us to become like little girls again, remembering our play and adventures. When Adah joined me in making a thank offering to Astarte, we could not help giggling, remembering the time we had offered her a sheep of mud. In between we were both happy to doze and eventually to drift into a deep sleep through the night.

She began the journey back to her own home the next day, escorted by some of Uncle Ruel's servants and bearing hopes for a healthy birth. She also carried a supply of food that Job insisted on sending with her. At first, she seemed a little insulted until we reminded her of the law of hospitality. I wondered why she reacted the way she did, but Job seemed to understand.

"Adah did not want to accept charity from us. Think of it, we do have so much more than Narmer's family does." Job was generous, not only in giving, but in tactful understanding.

Uncle Ruel was not allowed to enter the women's tent, but when I finally emerged from my confinement, he was right there waiting, with one of his big hugs for me, and the gift of a gold bracelet. Primus was by no means his first grandson, but he seemed as happy as if this were a first for him.

My father was happy too, mostly because he was relieved that I had survived well, and his new grandson was healthy and lovable. The wealth, so to speak, was Uncle Ruel's, but the gain of loving offspring belonged to both of them. I was a very fortunate woman.

It was almost two months later that I received word from someone passing through our town that Adah had given birth to a healthy boy. I was delighted. We were two friends making our way through life together, though apart. I left immediately to join her in celebration. Job and I prepared bags of gifts for her and the baby and I rode off escorted by a couple of Job's sisters. I was particularly pleased to be bringing a lovely blanket I had woven especially for Adah's child.

Approaching Narmer's tent, I felt a twinge of old, slightly painful, but happy memories of childhood days. My whole body trembled with excitement in anticipation of being with Adah. As the camel knelt, a smiling Narmer came to assist my dismounting. Adah appeared behind him, looking happy, and maybe a little surprised, as she embraced me.

"Dara. I am so happy you have come. Someone must have told you I had given birth."

"Of course I came as soon as I heard. How could I not

have been happy for you, Adah, anxious to see your first-born, and eager to bring him gifts?"

She received our offerings with polite and rather formal thanks, giving special favor to the blanket I had made.

"How lovely to have a gift of your own making. All the others are nice and appreciated, but they come from Job's wealth. This comes from your heart and hands."

I settled cross-legged and watched as she prepared tea, seeming more relaxed somehow as she set about that familiar task. Having welcomed me to his home, Narmer left us to fill the air with our reminiscent chatter.

Adah brought up the memory of all the times I had been annoyed with my mother because she wanted me to card or spin when I wanted to weave.

"Remember how good you were, Dar', at angry outbursts? They were funny to watch, though a little scary, and not at all nice when I was the object of them."

I did not understand how the topic of anger was raised so quickly on my arrival, but it did lead us into the pleasure of recalling our childhood.

"I guess I was too prone to anger, Adah, but I think partly it was because I had a strong sense of fairness. And in a way, I suppose my mother encouraged me, because she usually took the time to find out what was behind my outrage."

We drifted into reminiscing and laughing about our early years. I loved my life with Job and my new family and friends, but there would never be anything like what Adah and I had shared.

Adah was no longer in confinement, so I did not get to sleep alone with her as she had with me. She had returned to Narmer's bed. But there was a warm welcome for Job's sisters and me to sleep in the women's portion of the tent.

Over the evening potage and before our departure the

next morning, Adah and I had time together to share more of our stories with Job's sisters. I left feeling nourished with the love of an old friend.

I returned to a household pleasantly changed by Primus's birth.

Our lives became more centered in our own tent, and for a while the skills I had learned in growing up were put to use again as I prepared the evening potage, swept the tent, and even sometimes milled the flour. There was comfort for me in that.

The return to my earlier way of life, however, lasted only a brief time as years passed and our family and responsibilities continued to grow.

True to my heritage, I was good at childbearing. During the following years I birthed five more healthy children, two of whom were twins.

I received the help of all the people who were involved in raising our children as the way things had always been. I only vaguely realized that wealth and power were becoming an accepted way of life for Job and me, not just a sharing of his father's wealth.

For our firstborn children, the services of the wet nurses had been gifts from Job's parents, freeing me to engage in the business of our family and allowing my body to prepare itself for further pregnancies. Increasingly, our own servants cared for our later children. Our whole household, family and servants alike, was like family, largely because of Job's kind and tactful influence. Maybe it was our tribal background, but it never occurred to us to treat any people as less valuable than we.

That does not mean Job was ignorant of the possibility that there are those in the world who mean us harm. Soon after he was accepted into the Council of Elders, he was given the task of overseeing preparations for our protection from marauders. Along with the distribution of justice, security was a primary concern for the Council, which met more and more frequently in our home.

There I witnessed the high respect in which Job was increasingly held.

There was no doubt that Uncle Ruel and Job were major powers. That was confirmed for me when Uncle Eliphaz and other leaders would travel long distances on occasion from adjoining nations to engage in consultation meetings. Eventually Eliphaz, along with Bildad and Zophar, two other sovereigns from neighboring countries, became fast friends as well as colleagues.

My Job was the most highly respected of men.

7

Growth, Change, And Crisis

As Job climbed in stature, our daily lives departed ever more from the practices of our childhood until we came to bear almost no resemblance to the nomads we had been. Even our clothing was different, daily as grand as it had been on our wedding day. My flowing, lavishly adorned sleeves reflected the wealth of a woman who no longer did the basic chores of sweeping, milling, baking, water-carrying, cooking, planting, or harvesting.

The gains were many and wonderful, but each move forward in our position reflected the loss of the nomads we once were.

There had, however, been very little opportunity to mourn the tasks that had defined my early years, because as Job's responsibilities changed, the daily administration of our wealth fell to me. There would be periods of time when I traveled out to supervise the servants caring for our herds, or to consider the purchase of new pieces of land. I examined flocks of sheep and goats, donkeys, even camels, for potential purchase, bringing the information and my recommendations home to Job. There we made a joint decision.

The dispensation of charity became primarily my charge and pleasure, however. The law of hospitality flowed smoothly beyond entertaining visitors to doing well by all who could gain by our generosity. My mother-in-law had taught me well to carry it out with tact and appropriateness.

One familiar task from my early years did remain: the pleasure of weaving the materials that we used not only for our family, but also for the entire household.

Our children were rarely taught in the nomadic way when accompanying Job or me as we went about our work, but often our servants brought them along as they carried out their duties.

As for more formal training, the children of the extended household were the focus of care and tutelage equal to that received by our own offspring. For more sophisticated education, one of our best acquisitions was a brilliant slave who became the teacher for the older children.

Job and I did, as my mother had predicted, respect each other enough that we made our opinions known when we had our differences. Our arguments were filled with energetic strength of opinion, and they did not end easily. We usually persisted, often with loud anger, until we had worked the problem out, bringing it to a good resolution.

As our marriage and living situation matured, we were surprised by unanticipated arguments that forced us to accept that major alterations in our living conditions were required. I was more resistant than Job to impending change, but it was a struggle for both of us to accept the truth of what we had to do.

As our wealth and responsibilities had grown, so had the size of our community, requiring the addition of many rooms to our tent and more ample living space for the assemblage of servants and caretakers that now surrounded us.

Uncle Ruel's flock had been growing, as had Job's, so an extension of grazing and living space was required. In addition, Job's abode had become a focus not only for the meetings of the Council of Elders, but also for their administrative activities, requiring more appropriate housing for their work.

Therefore, with some regret, we made plans to move

our people and our animals to a location some three days'
journey from Uncle Ruel to a shelter and space that would
fill our needs.

So began the long project of planning and supervising
the settlement of our new locality.

Once I had accepted the necessity, I was eager for the
move to our new place, even proud of the success that led
to this change in our lives. But I was sad about leaving
the tent where Job and I had begun our lives together. I
would forever cherish my first sight of its location, the
undulating rise in the land, the acacia trees drinking deep
from below the sandy surface, the joy that wrapped me in
delight at first sight.

Only if I could feel that way about our new abode would
excitement in the new situation fully overcome wistfulness
for the past.

Two attempts to locate the ideal placement for our
household yielded nothing even close to that joy. Then,
on the third, as we crested a hill, my camel and I swayed
as if in response to imaginary music, with my heart directing the beat. On this spot Job and I would put down new
roots, embraced by the trees, the shadows, the color of
excitement and love.

Together my husband and I walked about, even danced,
taking in the view from every angle. With a joyful, loving,
and confident embrace, we began to trace the exact placement of our new home. Our vision imagined the walled
city that would grow around our dwelling place. I hesitate
to say palace.

What our eyes had conceived began slowly to become
real. Workmen swarmed about, skilled hands wielding
their tools, raising buildings. Animals struggled back and
forth, drawing their heavy loads of stones and, occasionally,

copper finishings. Women carried food and water to the laborers. Children played underfoot, often being shooed away by their caretakers.

Job and I received frequent reports from the overseers who traveled back with their information, drawing progress images in the sand. We traveled to the site as often as possible, my heart seeming to move in rhythm with the activity. A long period of our lives was devoted to the construction of our city, but finally the toil, the waiting, planning, and anticipation ended.

It was complete.

Our house was built of solid rock with a huge atrium in the center, shielded by large copper doors, ornamented in bronze. Around that entrance hall in a U shape were rooms on the main level and two balconied floors overlooking the atrium. The space on the main level was to be used primarily for activities of the Council of Elders. The upper balconies offered rooms for our children, their caretakers, and our most honored personal servants. There was always ample space as well for other travelers who might join us in the tradition of hospitality.

After those many months of work and anticipation, seeing our completed home was, as I had hoped, as joy-filled as the arrival at our marital tent had been. This time I was surrounded by an excited crowd of children and personal servants, dismounting to dance in delight as my family had done on that day so long ago.

I had chosen to leave without Job, who had stayed behind to supervise the dismantling of the tent that had surrounded us with affection for so many years. Even in the midst of our happiness, the thought of so much of my life being reduced to neat piles of tent material watered my eyes in spite of themselves.

As our children and their caretakers clambered about investigating the site of their future lives, we were greeted by a jubilant, jostling crowd of townspeople bearing garlands of flowers and baskets of fruit, vegetables, and herbs.

For some time before our permanent arrival, they had occupied the new city of smaller four-room stone structures within the walls. Each abode included storage rooms, food preparation areas, and space for their personal animals. Wells and cisterns were already nourishing gardens bursting with food and flowers of multicolored beauty.

The stone buildings themselves seemed to pulsate with hues, varying from mottled gray to pink, almost mauve. Sometimes the sun-reflecting textures gleamed so bright they appeared to be white, or luminous yellow. The gardens provided varieties from red, pink, blue, and white to silver and deep purple. And, of course, there were always different fragrances depending on the season.

When the celebrations were over and we were left to settle into our rooms for the night, I found myself still quivering with movement that did not want to stop. Our whole household seemed to be in tune with the same vibrations. And I missed Job. Sleep resisted me for some while, but was deep once it yielded.

On the first day in our new home, I awoke somewhat earlier than usual, with an unfamiliar excess of energy, dined on wheat bread and fruit, and rode out alone to survey our city and the needs of its people.

A touch of nostalgia surprised me as I found myself remembering the distant day when my mother-in-law introduced me to my new role as Job's wife. So much had changed since then.

In the silence of the ride, quiet thoughts flowed into the forefront of my attention. Even the donkey that bore me on its back seemed pensive as I savored the opportunity to slow down after the rush of activity that had consumed us during the past years. Happy anticipation had become reality. In a few days Job would complete his tasks at our former location and join me here, to sleep in each other's arms again, happily celebrating our new home. My mother had been right. I did enjoy our "potage" love.

I rejoiced in the many blessings enriching our lives, but my body languished a bit with strange sensations akin to hunger. The completion of the busy planning and work leading to the move to our new home plunged me into a period of quiet which I filled with contemplation of that which I had left behind. Yes, the donkey was right when he turned his head back as if to inquire after me. I was crying, not in regret, but in bidding farewell to a happy past.

Even as my cheeks moistened, I was struck with a realization that did evoke a sense of present mourning. I would have to travel a much greater distance to be with my own parents, or even Job's family. The way would be even longer to Adah. How I missed Adah. My chest began to ache with a longing to see her and share my joy.

When I had completed my day's expedition, I left my donkey companion in the care of a servant and returned to our rooms, set up my loom, and began to weave. The fabric begun that day reflected the nostalgia of my mood, but eventually the products of my creative labors changed in design and color. Job and I were together on a regular basis. The frequent travels and supervision decisions had accomplished their purpose, and I took great pleasure in the new location.

As seasons passed from planting to harvest, from sowing to reaping, our home no longer seemed new. We settled into a daily pattern familiar and yet modified in response to our changed situation. So busy were we that I failed to notice a strange reserve developing between Job and me. Our days together were still comfortably familiar. We embraced and enjoyed our potage love. Here, I conceived for the sixth time.

Sometimes, however, change occurs so gradually that we remain unaware of its growth.

As usual, being with child was a source of happiness, but toward the end of this pregnancy I found a strange mood wrapping me in shadow. Something was wrong, but I could not identify the problem.

Our marriage seemed to be changing in ways that I could not clearly describe and I felt a hopelessness that made no sense. Frequently I retreated to the privacy of the women's room, sacrificing to Astarte and pleading for her help.

Everything inside me had turned a dull gray that got drearier as I reviewed the possible source of this feeling. Occasionally I sank into reviewing my past. The answer must lie there, I thought, as I fell into the despondent belief that I had done nothing to make my life worthwhile. I had given birth to five healthy children, but any fit woman could do that, and other people were doing a fine job of caring for them.

I remembered my early lesson to do something useful when things seemed bleak, but even dyeing and weaving no longer gave me joy. My life was stretching ahead of me, just one long purposeless repetition of what I had already done which was giving no satisfaction to me or anyone else.

It seemed that Job had very little need for me, especially now since he was so involved in daily discussion with the group of men who met in our atrium or near the gardens, discussing I knew not what. It was not the Council of Elders, though Uncle Eliphaz often traveled to join them, sojourning in the guest quarters of our home.

Something about Job was changing. His face, even his body, seemed different when we were together, as if he were feeling uneasy, almost fearful, in my presence. Even as we shared our bed, he sometimes turned his back to me and pulled away. I knew not how to react to the change in his way of being with me. If he were upset with something I had done, he would have told me.

I longed to ask him, but for some reason I had lost my power to risk an argument, fearing where it might lead.

I understood his avoiding my body. That had happened in some of my previous pregnancies. But even then he had often given me a long and enthusiastic hug when it was least expected. This was different.

His presence felt ominous, like the desert storms I had sometimes experienced when no one else seemed to be aware of them.

He avoided arguing with me. Had he lost his respect for me? Had his love faded? It seemed he was sharing none of his experiences with me. Had he transferred his dedication to that group of men who were deeply involved in daily discussion?

When I asked what they were talking about with such animation, he managed to turn the conversation to another topic, holding something secret from me, which he had never done before. At the same time, I often noticed an air of joyful excitement in his demeanor when he was with those men.

Nothing made sense. All of it fed my belief that my life had lost purpose. I thought sometimes that I had caught Job's unease and made it part of myself. Had not my mother said, "An attack on his body will be an attack on yours and whenever he is spared, you will be spared. And he will know you in the same way."

Maybe this is what she meant. We have truly become one, so we share each other's emotions as well. Perhaps it was Job who was suffering storms inside. Perhaps he was so distant because he did not want to tell me how he was suffering. I longed for the courage to press him to speak.

But maybe he is just tired of me. He could be hesitant to tell me that he longs to take another wife. Perhaps he already has. No, he has not the time for that, being so busy with Uncle Eliphaz and the other men.

The whirlwind inside me was brewing into something beyond what I had ever before experienced. It was as if the gates had slammed shut and I was unable to release the turbulence confined within.

What had happened to the Dara who was so good at picking a fight? What had happened to Job and me that I feared accosting him with my concerns? I longed for a battle, carried to its conclusion until I understood what was happening.

My mother said she and my father argued because he respected her. Has Job lost his respect for me? Maybe that is why I am feeling so little respect for myself.

Maybe Job is feeling helpless and I am adopting that heavy feeling for myself. Maybe he needs me more than ever to help him through that torment. But why would he, so successful and powerful, be feeling helpless and useless?

I want to ask him.

I need to ask him.

I am terrified of his answer.

Again I retreated to my own quarters and appealed to Astarte for help.

One day, as I was trying to fulfill my daily obligations, the storm grew so intolerable that it broke through. The pain ruptured my fear. Hardly realizing what I was doing, I attacked Job with angry words when he came home from his daily meeting with those men who seemed to have replaced me as friend and confidant.

"This is more than I can bear, Job. Just what is going on between us? What is happening to our marriage? Have you taken a concubine? No, I think it is even worse; you are giving all your love and devotion to that group of men. I think there is something improper in that."

My voice trembled with angry tears that I could neither quell nor release.

"Our life is in no way like it used to be when we were young parents, or like I expected it to be when we married."

Some sensible part of me knew that was a ridiculous charge, since our lives had so long ago left our traditional roles behind. Yet I found myself standing more firm as I entered, albeit with trembling, into the sense of argumentative power.

"You are never in the fields or out with the herds. What are you doing anyway, spending all that time talking with those men?

"I am happy to do my share, as my mother used to say, but it is not at all like what I learned to expect in my home. Does it not even bother you that I am making most of the important decisions in our life? Do you not ever long for the old days? Just what is going on here?"

I could see Job flinching, as if I were hitting him. To tell the truth, I wanted to. That would have felt good—much better than the helplessness and fear I had been nurturing.

Job came right back at me, anger for anger, and that felt good also.

"So! You are too rich. Your life is too good. You do not have to do the menial chores, and you get to be in control of most of our life, even of our wealth. Do not pretend you dislike being in control. I have known you for a long time, remember? So what are you complaining about?"

"Job, you are avoiding my point," I said too calmly, holding tight control as I realized the truth of what I was saying. *I am not even sure what the point is. There is something wrong even with his anger. It seems impure somehow, or shallow, like a fragile cover on a container of fire. Oh, Astarte, help me. I am so frightened. This is not my Job.*

It almost seemed it was not rage he was feeling, but fear. This would not be the first time my anger seemed to frighten him, but now there was a different quality.

Then I asked him the question that broke through his discretion. "You must tell me, what are you doing day after day with those men? It is not the Council of Elders. You are not making important decisions for our nation. It is almost like you are in love with them. You cannot wait to join them every day. Is it because they treat you like you are so important? I guess I am not the only one who likes to be in control. What are you up to?"

By now I was trying very hard not to cry. All I wanted was to understand why my tears were straining to erupt, and why they would not.

"Dar'." Job's voice turned gentle, even as it yielded to trembling, just as mine had done. "It is not true you are making the important decisions. Yes, you have the major part in running our daily life and supervising our wealth. Our worldly situation depends largely on what you do. But what I am doing in my discussions with the men is really the most important for us and our position."

"I knew it, Job. It is all about your importance in this world. You really do like being the leader that all the men look up to. That desire has drowned all else in your life that was once important."

"No, Dar', that is not true. It is about God and how He watches over us."

What is he talking about? 'He watches over us?' But Astarte is not a male. What is he saying? What does this have to do with the way he has been treating me? Now he is confusing me. Perhaps that is what he wants to do. Is this his way of deflecting the argument? Astarte, help me to understand.

Job's voice was even more gentle, and firmer now, as if he were trying to protect me. From what?

"I have come to understand that everything we have is because He has given it to us."

He? Why is Job saying 'he?' Fear had grasped me in even tighter bonds.

"That is what we talk about and study every day. In a way, we have rediscovered a devotion which was abandoned by previous generations of our family."

Our devotion has been to Astarte. How can he say we have abandoned it? I certainly have not.

"Dara, listen to me. This is the most important thing that has ever happened to us, more important than each other, our family, our wealth, our tribe." His voice turned tight, as if his throat were trying to hold his words back even as they broke out of his control. His voice ground its way out almost silently as he pleaded with his eyes and his arms seemed to strain to prevent reaching out to me. "Please listen. This is why I did not want to tell you. I knew you would be hurt and dismayed."

Thank you, Astarte. At least he is finally talking. The urgency in his voice is strangely reassuring, but what is he talking about?

As if he could hear my thoughts, he went on, a little less tightly restrained.

"I am talking about the worship of the God of our ancestor, Abraham. You are right. I am in love, not with the men with whom I study, but with God. This God demands that we pay homage to Him and worship Him constantly, offering up to Him all our activities as a tribute. If we do not, His anger can be intense. Truly, because of my concern for you, I have not dedicated my whole self to Him as fully as I should. For that reason I am suffering great discomfort."

I was aware of a rare stiffness in my body. It was tightening painfully, ready to deflect the attack I felt coming. *Because of me? What am I being accused of? Now I am not feeling reassured at all. Something terrifying is happening.*

"I knew you were sensing my stress," he struggled on. "I should have unburdened myself a long time ago. Torn between my love for you and joy in my God, my days have been long and hard, but I did not want to hurt you."

Hurt me? How could this revelation hurt me? If Job has found such happiness with this god, why should it bother me? Why would he not share it with me sooner?

I found myself leaning toward Job, my body losing some of its tension. "Job, I can see that the men in this group are dedicated to spending more time with this god than one would ordinarily expect. He must be an important one. Even Uncle Eliphaz travels from afar to be with all of you. So, Job, that is all it is: another god to add to the help we already get from Astarte?"

I am relieved. Job has released his secret. I have been entertaining such frightening thoughts, but it is only the discovery of a new god. Now he can instruct me and we can go on with our lives, enriched by the knowledge of this additional protector.

Still, there is something in his face, in his eyes, in his whole posture. There is more, I think, and I am terrified of what it may be. Help me, Astarte.

Then he struck me with those terrible words.

"Dara, this is not just another god. This one insists on being the only God. All the others are false. Like Astarte, they are just man-made idols, no more than the doll you used to play with when you were little."

The look Job is giving me is more confusing than his words. Such sadness and sympathy, even love, infused with a fiery power and determination I have never sensed in him before. Well, perhaps that is not true. That fire may have been part of what was making me uneasy lately.

Now that the door had been thrown open, all that had been hidden within him came out, without hesitation or effort to be kind. Perhaps there was no way to be kind about this.

"Do you hear me? I have come to understand that Astarte is a false god. She should not be in our home, and we are offending God every time you offer sacrifices to her. I feel sinful and fearful that she is here. I feel guilty that I am hurting you. I am sorry, but she must be removed from our home."

Yes, Job was greatly distressed, even fearful. It was clear he had been holding back these words with a great deal of effort. Now they were released, breaking out like a fire that had been contained for too long. He reached out to touch me, thinking he would comfort both of us, I suppose. But I pulled away from him. The last thing I wanted right now was to be touched by him.

My breath was gone, but so was the bleakness. In its stead was a torrent of wild anger, confusion, defiance, disbelief …

Astarte who has protected me through my childhood, through fear and love, through betrothal and marriage, through five birthings, Astarte has to go? Job cannot possibly mean it. He could not be that cruel to me. His love for me would not allow him to do it.

He could not force me to remove Astarte. Of course he could not. I would not do it. Now I was crying, and I did not like that either. I never did like for anyone, even Job, to have such power over me. Caught between Job and Astarte? It could not be. Suddenly I was filled with terrible, undirected energy. I went looking for a broom to sweep the floor. I went to find Astarte. I ran outside. I sat at the loom and got up again. There was no place to stop. There was no comfort. I was furious, frightened, alone, powerless, and filled with angry energy. The love was over. Job had abandoned me.

I had to see Adah. I ran around in a disorganized gathering of what I needed for a journey to her. Job kept following me, doing and saying things that made no sense. He himself made no sense to me anymore. When he became aware of my intentions, he sent for Sophronia, my favorite maidservant, probably because she was so level-headed and competent, the way I was before this terrible thing scattered me to the winds.

Twisting his hands together, fear tingeing his voice, he instructed her "Prepare to be with your mistress wherever she goes and serve whatever needs she has."

Poor thing, she was having a hard time maintaining her usual calm efficiency when she saw the wildness in our behavior. Job summoned two of our menservants to go with us: Timon, who we both knew held me in particular honor, and Sergius, devoted to both Job and me.

None of that really mattered to me. I just had to get away from this place. I had to keep moving. I had to get to Adah. I slipped Astarte into one of my bags and mounted my donkey, ready to leave. It was a good thing Job saw to it that we were provided with supplies, because I was far too distracted to focus on our practical needs.

As we four were about to leave, Job held me back. With a look of devotion beyond what I had ever seen from him before, he said, "Dar', I love you. Do what you have to do and come back to me."

I want to believe the love you are declaring and even demonstrating, but how can I?

I wanted that love. I did not want his love. His declaration just added to the turmoil. To love Job I was being asked to give up my love for Astarte. I wanted to stay angry, though I did embrace him, out of habit, I suppose. I knew Job well enough to recognize that he was afraid I might choose Astarte over him, but I was in no mood to care about that.

The journey to Adah was longer and harder than I had remembered. This time I was pregnant. The heat waves rising from the sand slashed at me, searing through my clothing. The weight of the child inside me bouncing up and down as we rode was a rock ripping at my insides.

I wondered if my pregnancy diet, with no salt or fat, might have weakened me.

Maybe the hardest part was that the energy fed by my anger and shock eventually abated, and I was left with nothing but sad confusion and bleakness.

Job had been right to send servants along with me. I think my grief and dismay over having to choose between Job and Astarte would have been intolerable without their company. They were quite subdued, however, wondering what this sudden frantic trip was all about, I suppose.

I spent much of the journey holding Astarte tight to my body. Her presence did give me some comfort, but even she could not stop my ruminations.

My life will never be the same. My days of happiness and joy are over. I will never again be able to feel love for Job. This baby will be born to a mother out of whom all emotion has poured. Maybe it will not even succeed in being born. I am an empty shell, living from now on only out of habit.

The desolation of the desert we were passing through was nothing compared to the wasteland inside me. I could feel myself shriveling up in the dryness. I saw no color, neither in the flowers of the desert nor in myself.

On the first night Sophronia decided we should pause on our journey earlier than would ordinarily have been expected. I was not thinking clearly enough to recognize my own exhaustion and the danger to the child I carried, but I was ready to yield to her care. After a repast only a small part of which I ate, she and I lay inside the tent raised by Sergius and Timon who lay protectively outside the flap. Neither she nor I slept well. She was alert, watching over me as I lived out terrible dreams of being alone in the desert without water, a dried up old woman, tossed aside with no one to love or care for me.

I was even more fatigued in the morning than I had been when we retired for the night. The exhaustion that slowed me down in the next days' journeys did help me to sleep the following nights. That was a blessing for Sophronia who certainly needed her rest, but it did not refresh me at all. Each day I ached and slowed down more. Each day I clutched more desperately to Astarte.

Worse yet, I felt myself, my strength, my awareness disappearing into gray nothingness.

The usual three-day journey west to Adah's stretched almost into four, given the slow pace I was setting. For me, however, there was no time, just aching misery of body and soul.

Approaching the end of the journey, as I saw Adah's

compound emerging as an undulating blur in the distance, I faded away into blackness.

8

Home With Adah

Clutching Astarte, I collapsed off my mount into Timon's arms. As if from afar, I heard the dismay in Adah's voice directing him to carry me into the women's tent.

The odor of aging wool recalled feelings of childhood safety as Timon lay me on the rugs that had been spread for me. Through a quivering blue haze I felt cool cloths on my face and arms, gently applied by visions of Adah and Sophronia. Astarte lay on my chest. Safe at home with Adah and my goddess, I was comforted as I drifted into a deep sleep.

When I woke, I lay on the sleeping rugs, too heavy to raise myself. Confused, I touched the unbleached linen garment clothing me and inhaled the familiar moist, warm scent of mixed vegetables seasoned with fresh herbs cooking on the fire. How long had I been home? How had I come here? Was my mother expecting me to rise and assist her?

A familiar but mysterious sadness attacked me. Even as I strove to place myself in time and space, Adah pulled back the flaps and entered the tent. Her face was tight with what seemed to be an attempt to conceal deep fear. Kneeling beside me, she whispered, "Dar', are you feeling better? You have had a very long sleep."

Warmth flowed through me at the sight of my dear friend. I tried to rise to greet her with a kiss and an embrace, but the attempt was futile. I had no strength. "What is happening, Adah? Where am I? How did I get here?"

With a look of relief, she recounted the events of the many hours ago when I had arrived in Timon's arms. Asking

106

no questions of her own, she lay beside me, filling me with her strength. Our familiar unbleached attire comforted me. I was home, not with my parents, but with Adah. Memory tried to give comfort to the familiar, but where recollection might have been, I found only an amorphous nothingness.

"Will you take some refreshment?" Adah asked. "I have some ready for you if you have the strength to eat it." I wanted the comfort, but I was not eager for food and I did not believe I could move. "I will bring you some," she said, leaving the tent. When she returned she had a small bowl of potage, the aroma of which filled me with desire to partake of the familiar food, though my body was not eager to take in much.

"You need to eat some," Adah said. "If not for yourself, then for the child you are carrying."

The child. I'm pregnant. I reached to feel my abdomen. It moved gently in response to my touch.

Memories strove to creep back, still clouded by a curtain of concealment. I chose instead to drink in the sights and smells of the women's room. I recognized on the walls some pieces in yellow, blue, and even red woven by my own family. How close we had been.

Adah moved behind me to support my back as I sat to dip some flat bread into the potage. Patiently accepting my slow movements, she recounted equally slowly the way of my arrival.

"Your servants were extremely caring of you in spite of their own obvious exhaustion. It is clear they hold you in high regard. Just as clear was their fear for your welfare and their confusion as to the reasons for the journey. When we had you safe on your bed, I released them to the guest quarters, though they insisted first they must unload the supplies Job had sent. And Sophronia would not sleep until she had removed your travel soiled garments and clothed you in one of mine.

"Nor were your two male servants willing to cease working, although they did first allow themselves a deep refreshing sleep. Right now they are out tending the flocks with Narmer and my eldest son. Sophronia will not cease helping me with my chores. They have all, however, in the past couple of evenings, joined us in our family repast, seeming ever more comfortable."

Sophronia, Timon, and Sergius were safe and undamaged by the journey. For that I was grateful. More memory came back to me as I recalled the two menservants riding protectively close by my side and Sophronia sharing a tent with Astarte and me. Now Adah and Narmer were making them welcome in the tradition of hospitality.

We have been here several days! What has happened to me?

The grief attacked me again, though the cause of these events remained hidden.

Safe in Adah's care, I escaped again into sleep, waking occasionally to partake of some food.

I know not how long I had been with Adah on the morning when I awoke, sat up, and moved to join the sounds of family outside the women's tent. There was her daughter sweeping the tent, her youngest son carding wool, and the flat bread on the plate over the fire. Adah leapt to her feet, her face alight with welcome, rushing to fold me into her arms. "Dara, you have recovered. Come, join us for our morning meal." On Adah's signal her children came to me, bowing slightly before embracing me with a kiss on each cheek. Sophronia approached me as well, embracing me when I extended my arms in invitation.

I joined the family as if all were normal. It was almost like coming home to the familiar after a long journey into a life—my life—that had wandered so far from the accustomed path. Even as I settled into the contentment of the familiar, however, I felt my memory reaching in vain to introduce the thoughts and emotions of the events that had brought me here. Trying to ignore the developing pain, I wrapped some olives into the proffered flat bread and accepted a cup of water, anticipating the pleasure of filling my hunger.

I know Adah was aware of my only partially hidden distress, but, as good friends do, she refrained from asking questions. Our conversation, therefore, focused on her news.

She was clearly in the middle stages of pregnancy. Over the years she had presented Narmer with a family of three children, two sons and a daughter. Each time she gave birth I had gone to her immediately when travelers reported the news. She had always received me kindly.

"Adah! I see that you are once again with child. I am so happy for you. Do you remember how you joined me directly after my first birthing? Your presence made my joy complete. I am sorry I never got to your side soon enough to be with you in your period of seclusion."

I paused for a moment as I became aware of the fear and ache behind the question I was about to ask. Studying her face and forcing myself to be courageous, I tried to speak normally, but my throat tightened, holding the words to a near whisper. "Adah, I have always wondered why you never sent for me at the time of any of your three birthings."

Her face changed, though I cannot describe how: tighter, maybe, or with a pulling together of her cheeks. She smiled the kind of smile that did not include her eyes. Turning slightly away from me, she reached to flatten a turned-up corner of the rug on which we were sitting.

"Oh," she said with a strange smile, "I just cannot keep

up with you. This apparently is your sixth pregnancy. I guess you are winning the mother race."

Winning the mother race? What does she mean? I know I have been eager to give Job children, but I have never thought of it as a race.

"Adah, do you believe we are in a race?"

The corner of my vision grasped sight of Sophronia quietly leaving the tent.

"I was only joking, Dar'. I just hate to bother you when I know how busy you are."

Bother me? Is she avoiding looking into my eyes? I do not want to hear that now, even as I am struggling to find the cause of the terrible sadness I am experiencing. A memory struck briefly, attacking like a high wind beating against me. But I could not hold it. I knew only that I was struggling with Job.

Was I losing my husband and my best friend?

Lowering my head into silence, I gained strength to return my focus to Adah.

I found myself feeling again the brewing storm I experienced when I first brought Adah to see the tent Job was raising for us. Had I been creating a competition, flaunting my good fortune without realizing it?

Could it be that I have been in some kind of rivalry with Adah? I do not think so, but is that not what she is saying?

The thought caused my abdomen to feel empty, and the child within me to move violently.

Have I lost my best friend? I cannot let myself entertain the thought. Adah and I are too closely woven together.

Drawing her eyes to me by touching her arm, I pleaded, my voice trembling in spite of my efforts to control it, "Adah, my heart will break if you believe we are rivals, competing with each other. Our friendship is so important to me. You are entwined into the very essence of my body. I cannot imagine important things happening in my life without sharing them with you. Have you changed in your feelings for me?"

I saw the tear she tried to conceal. "Oh, Dar', of course not. How could we have gone through childhood and so many life events together and not now feel the same deep friendship?" I felt the love. So did she. We were on our feet, holding each other tight in mutual affection and dedication. Again I drew strength from Adah.

Doubts had been planted, but I had to shut the door on them. I could tolerate no more pain. I drew back into the comfort of the familiar, allowing myself to return to my childhood self, strengthened by Adah's care. The unremembered cause of the pain that had brought me here sank deeper into hiding in my abdomen, driving the child within to unaccustomed activity.

As days passed and my strength returned, I joined Adah in her daily routine. I went with her to the well to fetch water. We worked together milling the wheat chosen to honor my presence. We celebrated my return to physical strength with a visit to the market.

There was the clamor of marketers calling for buyers to sample their wares. The sight of yellows, greens, reds, whites, and browns reached for our eyes. The tangy smell of fresh fruits and vegetables, tinged by the odor of rotting fruit seemed sweet as it evoked my nostalgia. Many-hued rugs and coverings reminded us of the days when I brought my family's wares to market, a recollection that tightened my throat with regret for childhood gone. I think Adah was feeling the same way.

As we always had, we stopped to enjoy the bouquet of fragrant oils. We smiled with the recollection of the oil Uncle Ruel had given us for our dolls. Then we could only dream of the day when we would purchase oils for ourselves. Now it was a habitual task.

As in the past, our final stop was an examination of the jewelry we could only long for then.

"Your jewelry is finer than most of these pieces," Adah observed.

I thanked her for noticing. I wished I had left it at home.

The regret passed quickly as we danced arm in arm like children, arriving home with girlish laughter just as Narmer and his son, along with Timon and Sergius, returned from their work. Our happy presence seemed to light a glow of joy in the group. Narmer, followed by his eldest son, greeted me with an embrace and kisses on both cheeks. "How happy I am to see you fully recovered." Timon and Sergius looked like they wanted to embrace me as well, while Sophronia sent a broad smile from her position tending the evening meal that she had prepared in our absence.

Conversation was loud and constant as we dipped our flatbread into the pot like the huge loving family we were for the moment. Watching Adah and Narmer interacting with each other created a soft warmth within me. I had not known how kind and amusing Narmer could be as he seasoned our conversation with laughter. I could not remember the last time I had so enjoyed myself.

"Now," said Adah, "let us open up one of the pomegranates we purchased and offer it to Astarte in gratitude for this wonderful time together."

Silence imprisoned me. Then I broke forth into sobs from my very depths, sobs I could not prevent, nor did I want to. I had converted the joy of the occasion into astonished horror. Only Adah interrupted the picture of frozen fear and helplessness as she leapt to embrace me.

The full recollection and terror of all that had transpired with Job came rushing back.

"Astarte, Astarte." Tears and words rushed out unrestrained. "Job," I gasped. "He says I must cease my worship of Astarte."… "That is why I am here."… "I am so sorry to upset you." …" I have tried" …"to conceal the truth" …" from myself and you."… "But I can hold back my torment no longer." … " Job says I must remove my goddess from our home." … . "But I cannot stay with Job without Astarte." … "I cannot live without Job." … "I cannot live without Astarte." … I cannot live."

Sophronia , Timon, Sergius and Adah's children quietly left the tent.

"He commands the removal of Astarte"… "She must leave our home" … "She offends his jealous god"… "I must cling to no other god but his."... "something about the god of Abraham."… "He says our people worshipped this god in the long-distant past." … "He says we abandoned this god." … "He has rediscovered this god."

Are you telling me," Adah asked, "that Job insists you must worship only this god that he has somehow discovered, or rediscovered? Does he really mean you must abandon Astarte? But she has protected you through so many life events. Even this baby you are carrying. What will happen if you lose her care?"

Rocking back and forth in pain, I released my faltering words with a bit more calm. Knowing that Adah understood my agony reduced my frenzy somewhat. "The terrible thing is that Job has not stopped loving me. I know he has no desire to abandon me. In fact, I am sure he is frightened that I may choose Astarte. How can I renounce either one of them? It is hopeless. Sometimes I wish I could just go back to the nomad I was before Job accomplished such heights.

I can see no happy ending to this pain."

Focused on myself and Adah, I was only slightly aware of Narmer's presence in the background. He leaned toward me as if to offer comfort even as he remained in the position he had held when this outburst began.

Adah held me firmly in a long period of silence until my turmoil slackened.

Then suddenly she loosened her hold on me and pulled her body together in determination, turning to face me and grabbing the attention of my eyes.

"Dara, you must make a choice that will end this dilemma. You cannot allow yourself to remain in this terrible state. It must be either Astarte or Job. There is no middle road. Now, we must try to help you determine what direction you want to take."

Adah's words were harsh, as if she had struck me. If it was her purpose to end my immersion in pain, she had accomplished her goal. I found myself sitting up straighter, free of the mournful rocking.

But I do not want to sacrifice this pain. At least I am still connected to both Astarte and Job. If I give up the pain, it will be because I have made a choice. And I cannot choose. I love and need them both. I cannot do this. It is easy for Adah. She is not faced with this agony.

"But Adah, Astarte has not abandoned me. Only Job has done that. And I suppose that is not fair to say either. He did make sure I was protected on the journey here, and he did tell me he loves me and wants me to return to him. No, I cannot leave either of them."

Then the sobbing resumed, quieter now, less wild. I saw that I did have to choose. I could not.

I knew I had Adah's complete and deep sympathy. In

spite of her efforts to stop them, her tears were coming. It felt good that she was sharing my grief.

Then, settling deeper into her position opposite me, she changed the atmosphere somewhat by saying, "Job is not the only one adopting the religion of that one jealous god."

She has heard about this god? How can that be?

Narmer moved closer to us, with an expression that seemed to say "now I know something I can do about the situation."

"I have other friends facing the same thing," she continued. "It seems to be a kind of general stirring."

Somehow knowing that others had struggled with this same problem helped me. It seemed a little more like a matter that might be understood.

"As for me," Adah continued, "I cannot understand such a selfish god. I think I do not like him. Astarte has never been so greedy as long as she gets the sacrifices she wants."

"Adah, you are right. Astarte seems more love-filled and reasonable than this god of Job's."

Adah leaned toward me as if to command that I pay attention to what she was saying. "I have observed that some families, after careful consideration, transfer their devotion to that one god, but in those cases everyone seems to be at ease with it, so there is no contention."

Narmer nodded in apparent agreement.

So, some people truly desire to transfer their devotion to this jealous god. There must be something good about it. Of course there must be something good. My Job would not be so adamant if that were not true.

"So Adah, it seems that part of what is causing my agony is that Job has made a decision without consulting me."

Narmer almost smiled his agreement.

"Maybe I can understand how that happened. When I

think back on it, I can see that it came to him only gradually in his conversations with Uncle Eliphaz and those other men. Once he had dedicated himself to that god, it was too late to include me in the discussion. For him, there was no doubt left to talk about."

Narmer stood up, gathered three bowls, and filled them with beer, offering up the refreshment as he resumed his cross-legged position. Maybe there could be an end to the suffering. She and Narmer seemed to have more knowledge of Job's god than I did. I guess the similar challenges her friends were experiencing had provided her with more information than I had encountered.

"The problem with the god to whom Job wants to devote himself is that he is so masculine. What does he know about what it is like to be a woman? Bleeding. Birthing. Nurturing. What does he know about what you and I are experiencing right now in our pregnancies? How can he understand the love we feel for children who have grown in our own bodies? In fact, how can he know how it is to live under the rule of our fathers and husbands? True, you and I have been fortunate with the men in whose care we reside, but the fact is they could be treating us almost any way they wanted, and we would have no say in the matter."

How wise Adah had become.

"Yes, what you are saying may be true." Narmer had found the place to enter the conversation. "But do you think it fair to expect us men to be devoted to Astarte? What does she know about being a man? Has she had to take on all the responsibility for keeping a family clothed and fed and sheltered? Has she had to wonder whether his wife's baby is really his? Has she had to be excluded like an outsider when his wife was bleeding, or birthing, or nursing? Can she even understand that we never feel quite so loved by our children as their mother is? Has she had to feel shame for not being as rich as other men? Has she had to resist those urges to be intimate with a woman who is not your wife?"

Adah's spine was very straight now.

"You have wanted to bed some other woman?"

Poor Narmer. Surely he wished he had not said that, but it was helpful to hear a man's point of view. That happened very rarely with the way men's and women's lives were kept separate. Thoughts and curiosity were taking over the pain of my body.

"Of course, Adah. Did you not know that? It is somewhat difficult being faithful to you, especially when your monthly bleeding confines you, or after your birthings. Nor does it help knowing that nothing requires me to lie only with you. There is no mandate against my taking a concubine, or even another wife. Masculine gods understand that. In fact, they encourage us to spread our seed. I believe even this god Job has adopted promotes that, as long as we do not use another man's wife."

If what he was saying was true, then it was a tribute to Adah that she was his only wife. I think she was beginning to feel honored. I know I was as I thought of Job's constancy. And I thought of poor Jarna, married to that old man who already had other wives.

Despair abated and hope grew as this conversation went on. I loved Narmer's humor, and I loved having such an open discussion with a man other than Job or my father. I was also fashioning a solution. Perhaps I could keep my devotion to Astarte, but secretly, so it would cause no pain for Job. That way we could have both masculine and feminine protection. It occurred to me too that Narmer was right. Astarte was not devoted to Job's welfare as she was to mine. I began to feel sympathy for Job, neglected by my devotion to Astarte. Two gods, one masculine and one feminine. It was a solution worthy of thought. Astarte in the women's room where she could attend to us without causing trouble for Job.

Exhausted serenity settled over me. Pain and confusion were not gone, but hope had entered. So too had the family and servants returned, sensing, I guess, that the storm and need for privacy had abated. The brief balance of the evening passed in quiet conversation.

Adah bade Astarte a good night with a gift of the opened pomegranate she had offered earlier. That night I fell into a wakeful sleep, only partly comforted by Astarte's presence. As I changed positions repeatedly, I thought about my growing understanding of Job. I had a new appreciation for the turmoil he must have been experiencing as he struggled to bring this jealous god of Abraham into his life without causing strife in his family.

A sense of calm was still with me when I awoke in the morning, though my rest was not complete. Joining the assembled group, I found myself able to enjoy their company even as I continued examining my thoughts. I was warmed by my newfound sympathy for Job, though I was still discomfited by the fact that he could not fully worship this god to his satisfaction unless I joined him.

It still made no sense to me that his god demanded to be the only one. Why could he not be like the other gods we knew and just battle to keep his place with all of them? Aware that I was still trapped between my dedication to Astarte and my love of Job, I felt, however, that a resolution might be possible. Perhaps the secret worship of Astarte that had occurred to me the evening before, though I was quick to see the difficulty of living a lie.

How comfortable it was being with Adah and her family. It felt more real, somehow, than the life of power and wealth I had hardly noticed I was enjoying. An urge to journey on was, however, taking hold of me. I longed for my home and family, especially my children. My anger with Job was beginning to fade into a new understanding of his need for a god of his own. Yet I was not ready to return. I could not promise Job I would sacrifice my love of Astarte for the love of him and his god.

I found myself yearning for Uncle Ruel, believing he would be able to help me further in my effort to resolve this. Though I felt deep gratitude for the love and care of Adah and her family, I knew I must travel on.

The next morning I dressed in my own attire, freshly prepared by Sophronia, and took leave of my treasured friend and her family. The parting was tearful, but tears of a different quality. Tears of love and gratitude. Tears of regret at leaving their presence. Tears of hope that we would be together again soon.

Embracing Adah as if I would not release her, I said, "How wonderful it has been to be here with you and your family. It is the dream I had as child to be with you as we grew together."

"Truly," Adah responded. "Your presence has filled me with warmth, though I regret the terrible problems that brought you here."

"They were terrible, and still are unresolved and painful, but so much easier to bear since you and Narmer have given me hope that a solution lies ahead."

With his hand on my shoulder, Narmer stood behind me. "I wish you well on your journey. May the god you choose bless you on your way."

Reaching back to touch his hand in appreciation, I could

not release my hold on Adah. "Dear friend of my childhood, let us continue to share the joy of our lives. I long for you to come when this child I am carrying is birthed, and I pledge to come when your next is newborn."

"Dar', you know you continue to be as important to me as life itself. We will be together again. Our love for each other will not die."

And so we pulled slowly away from our embrace. I tucked Astarte into my travel bag. Narmer aided in loading our animals with an ample supply of food and water, pleased, I think, that he could treat us with generosity.

Sergius assisted me onto my mount as Timon assisted Sophronia. My three companions strove to hold back emotion as they parted with a family that had become a welcoming and welcomed part of their lives.

We four rode southeast toward Uncle Ruel.

9

The Wisdom Of Elders

Journeying toward Uncle Ruel's, my strength restored by my sojourn with Adah, I was acutely attuned to myself and our surroundings. My baby was still a heaving, jolting rock inside me, and the heat still slapped against me in searing waves, but I was not immersed in the despair and illness that had blackened my awareness on the route to Adah's.

I swayed with the familiar movement of my mount beneath me, and felt the cool comfort as we passed a watering hole. My eyes softened at the view of sheep and goats refreshing themselves there, along with their shepherd. The calm pinkish brown and black of the animals against the gray and silver of the ground, the blue of the water, and the cool shade cast by the two sycamore trees all washed me in serenity even as a part of me quietly carried the pain of my dilemma.

Sophronia, Timon, and Sergius were clearly reassured by the improvement in my condition. Timon even pulled out his reed flute and began playing soothing music, which led Sophronia and Sergius to join in song. After a while I heard myself singing as well.

Time passed almost without my noticing. Sighting the comfort of a small watering hole, we paused for a repast of bread and fruit that had been provided by Adah and Narmer. Refreshed, we rode on.

Now my body pressed forward eagerly in anticipation of the warmth I knew I would feel in Uncle Ruel's presence. As a child I had trusted in his power and care. Now memory carried me back to the excitement of those visits, and the stirrings of affection for his son Job. Job! My dilemma leapt to the foreground of my thoughts.

Job. Will I ever again enjoy his love? Maybe I can accept his god. Adah and Narmer have helped me see the possibility.

My thoughts reached out to Astarte for reassurance, suffering the realization even as I did so that she could not—would not—help me abandon her. In the confusion of my thoughts and the hunger for calm, I sensed the potage of care and counsel that would soon fill and restore me. But what if Uncle Ruel is not home. I was suddenly gripped with fear. I might be left alone with my torment. I do not have the strength to endure the emptiness of abandonment.

As his home became visible in the distance, hope and fear intensified. Hardly thinking of what I was doing, I removed Astarte from her case and pressed her to my breast.

Arriving at Uncle Ruel's was such a different experience from visiting Adah. It was not a tent we approached, but the doorway to a house that was much like Job's and mine, though a bit smaller. Like ours, the entrance revealed an open courtyard in the center, around which, in a U shape, were rooms. The lower rooms were for the household servants, while the family resided in the balconied upper rooms.

It was not just the structure that was different from Adah's tent. Being received by a servant was nowhere near as welcoming as the very personal greeting and intimate care Adah had given me. The warmth came, however, when Uncle Ruel gave me his wonderful hug. Like my father, he was aging a little, but still had his handsome power. My shoulders fell back into their place of comfort as my whole body was set free from dread.

"Dara. How happy I am to see you. We have heard from Job that you might seek us out." So, he had some knowledge of the conflict between Job and me. I found that comforting, especially as he personally escorted me to my quarters where necessities for my sojourn were already provided. As I enjoyed the ministrations of his servants and Sophronia, I decided there was no reason to withhold information from him.

Once I had washed and was reclining with the family around the lavishly appointed meal table, I plunged into the story of my dilemma. Sophronia and the menservants were being well cared for in the servants quarters, and I felt free to discuss these issues. My mother-in-law just listened, though it was clear she understood my distress at the threat of losing Astarte.

"I know," Uncle Ruel said, "this is a far cry from what you knew as a child. Everything about your life with my son is different from the nomadic existence you enjoyed when you were young. I can understand how important it is for you to hold onto something as familiar as Astarte."

I realized he saw the differences Job and I were experiencing as a reflection of the loss of my previous way of life. Was that it? Astarte was a symbol of who I used to be?

Perhaps that was true, but I wondered whether he really understood my love, devotion, and need for my goddess. I wanted to be sure he comprehended the depth of the conflict I was suffering. Feeling Aunt Beta's eyes drawing me to her, I looked at her with a concentration I had not granted her before.

She knows my struggle. She must have suffered this herself.

She said little, but the power of her sympathy fed my comfort and confidence. I was also receiving the care I had hoped for from Uncle Ruel, who was treating me with great respect. He could have simply ordered me to adopt Job's god. After all, Job had patriarchal authority over me. But that would not have been the Uncle Ruel I knew, the one who had taught his son such respect for me.

Instead, he seemed eager to help me understand the value of this deity. I realized as we talked that he himself had accepted that god of Abraham. He seemed firm in his convictions, but he did not try to lecture me. Instead he asked me about my adoration of Astarte. He asked me how often I sacrificed to her, or when she had helped me. My answer required careful thought.

"I certainly did cling to her when I left Job this time, so agitated in my despair. And I always turn to her when I am birthing a child. After all, she is a female. She understands. In fact, I have felt her loving and comforting touch when I was enduring the pain of childbirth. I even drew her to me as we approached your home today."

I reported to him and my mother-in-law my conversation with Adah and Narmer as we had discussed the difference between a feminine and a masculine god. Even as I said it, I realized I was referring to the distinction between a mother god and a father god.

"She was with me when I was betrothed and when I was married. In truth, I call on her whenever there is some kind of trouble in my life."

"And where is she now?" Uncle Ruel asked.

"She is standing on the floor by the bed you have provided." I found myself longing to fetch her as if she needed my protection. I wondered where he was leading this conversation, especially when I saw a look on my mother-in-law's face that suggested she knew what was coming next.

"So tell me, what is she doing while she is placed by your bed?"

I had the feeling I was about to be led in a new direction, one where I might be ill at ease, but I had to say, "Nothing. She is just waiting."

Then he paused. In the long silence, I began to understand that she was not always there for me, but only when I called on her. But how, I wondered, was that different from any other deity, waiting for our pleas to provide us what we need, and ready to be angry if we appealed to other deities to the neglect of themselves. This conversation was not helping. Now I had to be afraid that Astarte would be angry with me if I let Job's god into my life. She would not be good to me the next time I asked for her help.

"The God Job and I have come to worship is different, Dar'. He is always there. He does not wait for us to call on Him, but watches over us and takes care of us even when we are not aware of His presence. In fact, that loving and comforting touch you felt in the pangs of childbirth was the God of Abraham who blesses us even when we don't ask."

It wasn't Astarte who comforted me? That was more than I wanted to believe. But somehow I had to admit that this god was beginning to feel like my father and Job and Uncle Ruel all rolled into one. Maybe he was like a good father or uncle.

"But what does he know about women's things, like giving birth, or loving like a mother?"

"Oh Dar', He has given birth to the whole world, to all of us. Imagine how that labor felt, and the watching over everyone at all times."

I told Uncle Ruel I suspected giving birth to the world did not feel much like giving birth to a human baby. His argument helped me only a little. But he was persistent. He told me that another important thing about this god of Abraham and giving birth to us was that he created us in his own image. I took issue with that, too. Ruel did, after all, say "his" image.

"That is just a manner of speech," he said. "Of course

that includes females as well."

This seemed a little strange to me. "Then where can I go see him to know what this male-female god looks like?" I asked.

Uncle Ruel told me I could not see him. "In fact, God does not like it if anyone tries to see Him or make a statue of Him. You can only feel Him, just be aware of His presence."

"Then how do you know any of what you have told me is true? Does Uncle Eliphaz have something to do with it?" There, I had expressed my suspicions.

"Well yes, he does. He was the first to bring us the message. Actually, he reminded us of a message that has been with us all along, but our people have tended to forget it. Eliphaz restored a belief we should never have neglected. If you could see how excited he is about this, and how committed he is to God, you would be convinced too. His opinion is pretty powerful considering what a wise and respected elder he is."

This was feeling a little beyond my understanding. I glanced at my mother-in-law, hoping, I guess, for some signal of shared bewilderment, but it was clear she had come to agree with her husband. Is that my hope? Has she gone through the confusion about this new god and emerged comfortable in a belief in him? Or was she just yielding to Uncle Ruel's demand? I did not want to discuss it anymore. I certainly had not resolved my dilemma, but I did have many questions and much to think about.

We changed the conversation to stories of how my children were growing, and how my pregnancy was developing. Of course, it was now my mother-in-law who was most enthusiastically involved. Uncle Ruel just stayed quiet and listened. I could tell he had decided to give me time to think about what had been said. It was clear, however, that he was hoping to talk me into accepting this god who shares space with no others. I wished I could do that. It would have made it easy to be happy with Job again.

But even if I began to believe, I was never one to yield easily in an argument, or to admit that someone else was right. I had a lot to think about as I retired for the night on the soft mattress in the room I had all to myself. I was lonely, so I took Astarte into the bed with me and begged her to help me. Nothing happened. I pulled her closer to me, but I did not feel the comfort I had felt when I first left home, clinging to her all the way. Was she angry with me? I realized I was fingering the gold Astarte on the chain that Uncle Ruel had given me as a betrothal gift. It had become a common practice to which I gave no thought. No blessing flowed from the act. Had Astarte just vanished without a farewell?

A god who was always with me. One I would not have to tuck away in a bag, or pull out again in a crisis? I liked the idea. I wished I could believe. I had a question for Uncle Ruel the next day.

In the morning, Sophronia was waiting to attend me when I awoke. She seemed happy as she accompanied me to the presence of my parents-in-law, departing then to share time and food with Uncle Ruel's servants. The hospitality was there, but quite different from the traditional nomadic welcome Adah and Narmer had offered.

Uncle Ruel and Aunt Beta welcomed me with expressions of pleasure and hope as we reclined to break the night's fast with a lavish array of foods. Encouraging me to enjoy the pomegranates, Aunt Beta seemed to be honoring my devotion to Astarte. I think she was honoring my right to hold my beliefs if I chose to. An interesting lady, my mother-in-law. Rarely did she express an opinion directly, but always she managed to convey sensitive meaning with tactful gestures.

As the servants removed the remnants of our repast, I raised my question to Uncle Ruel. "What does your new god like in the way of sacrifice? "

"He likes burnt offerings, Ra', of sheep or goats or perhaps another animal, but never humans."

"I guess your god is not so different from Astarte, then. She likes sacrifices too."

He had no good reply for that one, except to acknowledge that it was true.

"But," he said, "Astarte and God are different in some important ways. First of all, Astarte is known as a household god. She serves only the family that accepts her as their personal deity, and then you cannot always be sure she will do as you ask. Think about it. Does she?"

I thought about the birth of my first child. How I had begged Astarte to spare me pain, but in truth the cramps were very intense. Uncle Ruel pointed out that Astarte acted on whim. Sometimes she would care for us and other times she would just ignore us. When you come right down to it, she is sometimes unfair in her treatment of us.

"Job's God and mine, on the other hand, is always just. He understands that people are not perfect. But as long as we work to obey His laws, He treats us fairly."

Uncle Ruel admitted that the God of Abraham, his God and Job's, does ask a lot. "He does expect us to worship Him regularly, not just when we need something, but the justice He gives us in return makes it all worthwhile."

"So," I wondered, "if I pray to Job's god when I am about to deliver this baby, can I be sure I will suffer no pain?"

"That is not the way it works with God," he told me. "It is in the nature of human birthing that there will be pain, just as men will have to work hard to supply food and shelter for the family."

Now I thought of Narmer's complaints about the requirements of being a man. And I thought of Jarna and her betrothal to the older man who already had several wives. Was Job's god being just? Would Jarna have been better off if she had worshiped Job's god? I raised those thoughts to Uncle Ruel.

He acknowledged that he could not pretend to know the answer to these questions. "I only know it is not the kind of day-to-day thing God is involved in. He has already created us with what we need to handle that. It is in the big things that His justice shows most clearly. No major harm will come to those who worship Him. And that takes us back to the sacrifices. Their purpose is to show God that you believe in Him and hope He will overlook any sins you may have committed. The idea is to make it clear that we understand that He is the all-powerful only God, and He is just."

Fairness was always a big thing with me. I could get very upset when things happened that were not just. Maybe I could like this god of fairness. It certainly would make Job happy. This god seemed pretty strong, and I liked that he felt like Uncle Ruel and Job and my father all rolled into one. But I would not lie about my convictions, either to Job or to myself, so I would have to think about it. If he was that powerful, it was hard to believe he was part female.

Uncle Ruel and my mother-in-law left me alone with my thoughts, responding to my occasional questions as I raised them. I sojourned with them for another three days, letting myself feel the strength of their understanding and protection. I hardly noticed Astarte still standing where I left her after the first night at their home.

All this thinking about men who took care of me led me to longing for my father. Suddenly I felt that I must see my parents, so I took leave of Uncle Ruel and Aunt Beta and headed northeast toward my old home.

I sensed the hope with which they bade us a good journey. I felt hopeful myself. Our mounts laden with gifts, we four headed on our way.

My emotions were not so divided as they had been on my way to Uncle Ruel's. I could not have explained why, but I knew deep down that everything would work out well, though I did not know how it could happen.

Now the familiar things we passed in the desert evoked nostalgic appreciation for my childhood home. There was a herd of camels, and fields of silver blossoms, and then suddenly the caves where Adah and I had enjoyed our winters near each other. I had heard people talk about being filled with emotion. Now I knew what they meant—the pleasant pain of a swelling heart.

Reminiscences flooded in as I approached my parents' settlement. I guess I was in the mood to reach deep into my childhood memories, because truthfully not much was different for me to notice in their home. I had been visiting them often, frequently bringing their grandchildren to see them. I suppose they were aging, but I did not notice it happening. They had not changed their way of living very much either, though they could have. My father's herds had multiplied over the years. That is what happens when you have good herds in the first place and care for them well. Multiplying is what they do. But my parents liked the way they lived in the midst of the tribe. My father's position was as honored as Uncle Ruel's, and I know he was proud of that. But aside from the luxurious rugs on the floor of the tent, more beautiful serving vessels, and a change of diet that included more costly foods, their life was as I had left it when I rode off on my wedding day. I felt comfortably at home, just as I had at Adah's.

This was not just an ordinary visit though, and over our evening potage I easily opened the discussion. I told them the whole story of Job's demands, my visits to Adah and to Uncle Ruel, and what I had learned in the process. My presentation was nowhere near as emotional as it had been on my other two visits. I was already feeling much calmer, and hopeful that I was finding a resolution to the Astarte issue.

On my way to them, I had practiced saying to myself, "This god is the only god. This god is the god of Job and Eliphaz and Uncle Ruel. Adah and Narmer have heard of this god, and they think it is acceptable that he is a masculine god. And Uncle Ruel thinks that females are created in this god's image too."

I had repeated over and over again, "Job's god is the only god. I can worship Job's god only," just to get a feel for it.

Would I be able to say it honestly? Would I be true to myself and honest with Job if I told him on my return that I had accepted his god? It did not feel completely right to me.

I needed to hear my parents' reaction, especially my mother's. After all, she was the one who had taught me to revere Astarte.

My father's response was immediate. "Of course you will adopt Job's god. Job is the head of the family."

I almost laughed. His response was so typical of the role of the commanding male, and so unlike my father who had always examined and discussed every major issue with my mother, even if it was true that the final authority was his.

My mother was smiling too as she embraced me. "No one understands better than I how devoted you are to

Astarte. Indeed, I feel the same way. But we have also been hearing about this movement to worship only that one god. In fact, we have been discussing it. While we are not abandoning Astarte, we have seen that others seem to blossom with happiness when they turn to this new god."

Until she said that, I had not realized that my body had continued to be tense even as I approached the home of my parents. Now I felt a massage of calm rolling through me. Even my baby seemed to quiet down inside me. We went on to enjoy the hospitality of my childhood home, sharing it with Sophronia, Sergius, and Timon. They seemed more comfortable than they were at first at Adah's when they were expected to eat and sleep with the family. I think maybe they were feeling easier too, sensing the atmosphere of increased ease about me.

That night my mother offered me her household Astarte, the one with whom I had grown up, to guard my sleep. I accepted; then I had two Astarte's by my side. As I lay there before drifting off, I realized that they were both statues. The real Astarte must also be invisible like Job's god. These statues were just representations of her.

I dreamt a lovely dream that night. I saw Job's god, a mixture of Job and my father and Uncle Ruel, embracing Astarte, and she returned the embrace. As if in marriage, she was becoming one with Job's god. Together they were one god.

I could go home happy to Job. My problem was solved. Maybe the joining of the god of Abraham and Astarte would not bear truth for other people, but for me it was a deep and moving reality. The feeling was still there in the morning. Astarte had melded into Job's god. I could have my masculine and feminine god, and the love of my husband. Ecstasy, relief, calm satisfaction, indescribable feelings of comfort all were mine.

We stayed with my family four more days during which I recited over and over to myself, "Job's god is the only god."

It became easier and easier. Every once in a while I told myself, "Job does not have to know I see his god embracing Astarte."

While I was there, I became increasingly aware that the child inside me was hoping to be birthed soon. I warned my mother that I might be sending for her as soon as I got home.

Before I left, I wove a blanket like the one my mother had made for my doll years earlier. I lay my Astarte in straw and said goodbye to her. I thanked her for being the wonderful companion who watched over me, wrapped her in her blanket, and placed her carefully in a woven box my mother provided for me. As a parting gift to her, I laid the gold betrothal chain around her neck, crying as I parted with the touch of Uncle Ruel. I told her I knew she had become the feminine part of Job's god.

When I got home, I would put my doll in there with her and store them both in a far corner of the women's room. I was at peace, and eager at the same time to return home to Job and my children.

10

Blessings At The Altar

"Job's god is my god. Job's god is the only god. There is only one god. Job's god is the one god." The words felt less strange and more calming as I repeated them. But often my thoughts and emotions strayed to a sharp awareness of my body astride my mount.

Excitement, eagerness, and even fear were coursing through me. I found myself rejoicing in a newfound freedom from conflict even as my unborn child was demanding release as well. The heavy weight had become a prisoner fighting to be free. What if this journey had been too stressful for the little one? What if I gave birth here in the desert? I wanted to be home. I wanted to be with Job. I wanted to see my children. I wanted to tell Job the good news. "Your god is my god."

As we approached home, my body struggled to keep my sixth child safe in my womb. Relief and joy set me free when we arrived at the city gate. Job was there, his face softening almost to tears. Pulling me gently but eagerly off my mount, he enfolded me in a long embrace, proving that a "figs and pomegranates and special cheeses love" can supplant "potage love," even after all these years.

There was another life, however, demanding attention. As if with a sigh of relief strengthened by eagerness, our baby was demanding to be free of confinement. I could not avoid attending to the recurring tightening of my abdomen and pelvis. Pulling away from my husband, I seized his eyes with mine.

"Job, I want you to receive this baby."

I did not give him the opportunity to resist. There was no time for that. I led him into the women's room and almost completely without pain delivered a beautiful baby girl into his hands. I was sure her birth was a message from Job's god. Narmer had complained that men were excluded from birthing. Now my Job had been part of it. I felt it was a special gift to him from me and from God. Job named her Nefer, which means "beautiful." Throughout her life he never stopped adoring her in a special way.

Shortly after the birth, Sophronia tapped on the entrance to the room, preparing to aid my body in releasing all that came after Nefer's departure from my womb. With her was another maidservant carrying the necessary linens and oils to care for the baby.

Job, holding Nefer, unmindful of her coat of water and blood, seemed to consume her with his eyes, often turning to me with a look that revealed awe and disbelief. For a man thoroughly familiar with animal husbandry, he seemed to be stunned by a strange combination of the familiar and the completely new. This was his own child he had received from his own wife.

Sophronia's entry seemed to make no impact on him, so it befell to me to urge him, as gently as I could, to leave us before the next stage in the birthing, even though I ached for him to remain with me. This was, after all, the women's room, and we were about to perform functions that belonged out of the view of men.

As if tearing Nefer from his own arms, he gave her over to the maidservant's care and backed out of the room, gazing at his daughter and me with a gentle radiance that spoke more joy than either of us was accustomed to tolerating. I have no doubt he went immediately to cleanse himself and to submit an offering for the sin of having entered the women's room. I was equally sure it was worth it to him to have broken tradition.

There had been no time to notify my mother or my mother-in-law, so Sophronia, supported by the energy of youth, overcame her own travel fatigue to provide the kind of loving care my family would have given. It was as if my kindred were there with me. I realized with a shock of comforting warmth that she and I were no longer just mistress and servant. What we had experienced during the pain and eventual relief of our travels had woven us together in a pattern of beautiful affection.

Sophronia was understandably fatigued, but her movements were quick, almost like a dance of excitement. Her body seemed to pulsate as she went about her efficient care while joyfully reporting the news of all that had gone on in our absence.

I guess Job felt relieved as soon as he unburdened himself of the secret he had been keeping from me. When I left he had made arrangements for the men of the household to be circumcised. He and our sons had their foreskins removed first and Job offered them up in sacrifice.

"Sophronia, this is terrible news. Can it be true that this god I have decided to accept requires such terrible evidence of devotion to him? I am not sure I would have made that decision had I known."

"Indeed it is apparently very painful, " Sophronia replied. "Timon and Sergius, having shared with you the journey of discovery, volunteered to submit their devotion to this one god, choosing to offer up their foreskins. Now they are lying in pain, waiting for recovery."

I noticed the other maidservant in the room seemed to hold Nefer closer to herself as she uttered a little cry of distress.

"I believe the other men who have been required to submit to this ritual would probably not hold this god deep in their hearts," I said.

Bending close as she finished cleansing my body, Sophronia responded, "I do not know about the other men, but the two who traveled with us are sincere in their acceptance, as am I."

It was then that I noticed her hesitation in addressing me as her mistress. It reminded me of the way Job and I had circled each other on the day of our betrothal. It was a strange but very acceptable feeling, which signified a new relationship. We were equals in the eyes of Job's god. For the moment I let the feeling stir the air between us with pleasing warmth.

"And what a wonderful surprise you will enjoy when you emerge from your seclusion and see the sacrificial altar that has been under construction while we were gone. It should be completed by the time you withdraw from the women's room."

"Oh Sophronia, describe it to me."

As if drawing a picture, she ran her hands over the wall. Extending her arms over her head and stretching to her full height, she said, "It stands at the highest pinnacle of the hill overlooking the city below." Then, bending deep down, she continued, "A solid base of earth and stone has been formed." Rising gradually against the wall, she described steps of rock leading to a terrace on which a frame of acacia wood had been built.

"Within the frame are heaps of rocks supporting a constant fire maintained by burning oils. One servant is assigned specifically to the task of replenishing the oils. Frequently he removes the ashes that have been formed and sets them in a pile beside the altar, as further offerings to Job's god. He volunteered first to be circumcised, so it seems his dedication is more than just a duty."

And there she stopped in her description. "Tell me more," I pleaded.

"The rest is still not finished," she said, looking pleased, I think, that she knew something I was yet to have the pleasure of discovering for myself. "It is best if you will be content to look forward to seeing it when you emerge from your seclusion."

Eager to explore this new world created by Job's god, I found the days spent in seclusion seemed longer than ever before. Indeed, they were longer as required by our God because I had borne a girl. I enjoyed the period of peace and quiet, but my longing for Job's presence was stronger than it had ever been.

Left alone, I thanked Job's god repeatedly. After a while, I realized I was no longer saying "Job's god," but simply "God." I did not think God minded that I had seen Astarte in his embrace.

On the day I emerged, Job took me directly to view the sacrificial altar. Throwing up my hands, I stepped back as if stricken by sun too bright to endure. It had a façade of gold leaf, mingled with silver and bronze, sprinkled with precious carnelian of blood red, orange, peach, and pomegranate rose, along with agate combinations of black, brown, and milky white. Those gems on my wedding sleeves had been beautiful. On Job's altar they recreated heaven on its brightest days, almost blindingly reflecting the intensity of the sun. God was present there in all His majesty.

When my eyes were better able to tolerate the light, I approached to touch the elegance of the precious stones implanted in the façade. I thrilled to the sense of heavenly music playing on my palms in response to the cadence of the rising gems. I felt the presence of God flowing into me through my hands.

I stepped back to review it again from a distance. Taking Nefer from Job's arms, I held her facing the altar, calling for God's blessing upon her, placing her so she could consume its beauty. My attention was then drawn to the terraced access to the altar where Job had our cultivated flower gardens expanded to the hillock leading to it. They were new growth that would explode in intense blues, reds, yellows, and oranges as they matured, just as our devotion to God would magnify.

But I had something to confess to Job. Returning Nefer to him and grasping his arms tighter than I intended, I told him, "Yes, I feel wonderful joy and adoration, but I am also very angry with God for causing you men to suffer the pain of circumcision. What sort of requirement is that, coming from a god who is supposed to be loving and caring? Worse yet, I feel confused and guilty because I am thinking those thoughts."

"Have no fear, Dara," he said, smiling, caressing me with a look because his hands were full of the baby. "It is acceptable to be angry with God. It shows how much faith you have developed that you are free to be outraged without fearing He would abandon you." Again I thought of the way I felt with Job and Uncle Ruel and my father, the assurance I had that they would love me and care for me no matter what.

I was seeing the advantage of being a woman, however, when the majority of the men of the city went through the same procedure. Once again Job offered up the foreskins in sacrifice to God. In fact, Job was sacrificing to God almost every day. He seemed overjoyed that he could finally be so public with his belief. It was also important to him to share the blessings of his devotion with all the inhabitants of the city. As time passed, he would occasionally sacrifice sufficient animals to have a feast for the entire community.

As I look back, my first view of the magnificent altar was a kind of beginning of a new period in our lives.

Nefer continued to grow, healthy and calm, undamaged by the terrible journey she had taken with me in my search for Job's faith. I felt particularly close to this little one after what we had been through together and nursed her for a full four months before yielding her to the wet nurse. I did not want to give up the thrill of her little mouth drawing on my breast, but I had to think of becoming pregnant again to enlarge our family further.

I began hoping for word from Adah that her time had come. I would have loved to be with her in the birthing. Finally I could wait no longer, so I sent Sergius to her. I told him to take with him whomever he needed, and I sent fifty goats and a pair of donkeys as a gift, a thank-you gesture for the help Adah and Narmer had given me on my distraught visit. Mostly my mission for Sergius was to bring back word of Adah's newborn.

Sergius returned with the goats and the donkeys and word that Adah had indeed borne a healthy baby boy about a month ago.

"They thanked you for the gift, but refused to accept it, asking me to deliver the message that they had no need for charity."

What have I done to bring this pain upon myself? Once again Adah has given birth without including me in the joy. And she has refused to accept my gifts. What has happened to our deep friendship? Have I offended her?

For some reason I could not identify, the vision returned, unbidden, of her comment regarding the beauty of my jewels.

I can see no reason why she would reject my offerings of gratitude, yet it seems clear that I have offended her. But how? Maybe I should not have imposed myself on her and Narmer when I was so upset about Job's god.

I just cannot bear the loss of Adah. I've got to see her and Narmer to explain that the things I sent were meant as an offering in exchange for the life-saving gift of hospitality and counsel they gave me in my time of need.

Maybe they do not understand they saved my life. Maybe I have not really understood it until now. I must go to Adah's.

Job blessed my journey, and blessed Sophronia and Sergius on their journey to accompany me. But he refused to allow me to take the gifts back to Adah and Narmer. He said he did not want to humiliate them. With his example, I was beginning to understand the discomfort Adah and Narmer felt as our riches seemed to separate our two families. When I visited them, I was returning to the familiar. When Adah thought of coming to me, it must seem like a journey into another world, one where she may feel she does not belong.

Just before we left, I changed my clothes. Now it did not seem right to be wearing my usual under-garment with intricately woven full sleeves. I changed into a sleeveless ankle-length linen tunic with a brown sash and a deep brown robe over it, more like our tribe's daily wear. I removed much of my jewelry too. My understanding had grown that my wealth was offensive, or at least uncomfortable, for Adah and that trying to share it only made it more distasteful.

As Sophronia and I rode off together. I knew Job was planning to go immediately to offer a sacrifice to God. It would be his way of protecting us. And she and I did have a good journey together. We had forged a special relationship

141

enriched by the emotional hazards we had shared.

So it was that we spent the trip talking about Timon. 'Talking' is probably not a good word for it. I spent my time listening to her adoration for the man. Thinking back, I realized the things I might have noticed had I not been so removed from ongoing events as I focused on my own distress.

"If he and I had parents in this country, I would be asking them to arrange our marriage."

With all our charity for others, I had been oblivious to the pain many of our servants must feel, having been torn from their own tribes in distant countries and brought to us to serve. As we rode our separate mounts, it was not possible for me to reach out and embrace her, but I hoped my words and expressions conveyed the understanding I was feeling.

"If you and Timon accept it, Sophronia, Job and I will arrange your marriage."

She pulled her mount into a sudden stop almost directly in front of me, looking like she intended to dismount. I was afraid she was about to kneel in thanks, a humiliating sight that would have pained me. Sophronia was my friend with whom I wanted to ride side by side.

It did feel customary, however, when she addressed me, "Mistress Dara, I will be forever grateful for that wonderful gift."

"And," I said, "I will be forever grateful for the care, comfort, and company you provided me on our long and stressful journey together in search of Job's god."

Pulling back, she settled in to ride by my side. "I assume Timon knows of your desire and would concur in plans for marriage?" I asked.

As if she could hardly make herself stay on her mount,

she assured me," Oh yes. I know it." I remembered dismounting and dancing on my trip to see the first site of my marriage tent. It delighted me to know Sophronia was feeling that same joy.

Time passed quickly as we made plans for her marriage feast, wrapping ourselves in excitement that dulled our attention to our progress, so the sight of Adah's camp in the distance came almost as a surprise. I think it was hard for both of us to put our conversation aside as we pulled up in sight of Narmer's tent.

When Adah saw us riding into her camp, her expression was strange. She seemed to be happy to see us. At the same time she looked behind us suspiciously, as if she feared we had brought back the gift of goats and donkeys. When her eyes scanned empty space behind us, she smiled, approaching me with a warm embrace, and Sophronia as well. Her body relaxed as if in relief when Sergius unloaded only a few baskets, containing the traditional foods expected when paying a visit.

Her smile was even broader as I opened my personal pouch and pulled out the baby blanket. It had become a tradition that I brought her a new woven blanket for each baby. "Oh Dara, I so love these gifts for my babies, woven by your own hand. They bring back such wonderful memories every time you give me one."

Narmer appeared quickly by Adah's side, moving to assist me in dismounting. Kissing me on both cheeks, he commented, "Dara, you look wonderful. What a pleasure to see you healthy."

"Narmer, my thanks go to you and Adah. Do you realize you saved my life?"

He acknowledged the truth with a quick pat on my hand. "Come in. You are always welcome."

And welcomed we felt. Sophronia and Sergius had no trouble settling into an atmosphere they had once found strange and uncomfortable.

On the first evening, sitting cross-legged around the fire pit and enjoying the potage with the flat bread, I again found myself nostalgic for the familiar, and when Adah suckled her beautiful new baby, my own breasts swelled with aching yearning to put my own little one to my bosom.

I guess it would not be right to say I was jealous, but I was, in a sense, grieving for a nomadic past that would never return. My familiarity with my wealth and position had crept up on me slowly, and I was contented with it. But it had meant the loss of the nomad I once was. Had I never left, I would be sitting here with Adah suckling my own baby.

At some point in the conversation I was able to say, "I wonder if you know how grateful I am for the way you cared for me the last time I visited here. I can hardly remember the state I was in when I arrived."

Narmer got up to fetch some beer for us, while Adah leaned forward, touched my knee, and said, with some urgency, "Don't you realize, Dara, that you are not a visitor here. My home always was your second home. This is the life you and I grew up with, the life we belong to, no matter how much things may change."

"Adah, you have put into words something that I only vaguely recognized. That is why I feel such comfort whenever I come here. In your presence, I know that the depth of our love has not changed. But there is something that troubles me. Why did you send back the gifts of gratitude I had sent to you? And why did you not send for me when you gave birth?"

Narmer had returned, distributing bowls of beer to each

of us. "You must know, Dara, that your way of life is strange to us. You have forgotten that there is a right way of gift-giving, just enough to show appreciation and not so much as to show superiority."

I did not know whether I wanted to hit or cry, or maybe both. "But it is also true that one wishes to share one's blessings with special friends. It made me happy to think you would enjoy what I sent you, knowing that it was a gift, not a sacrifice. A desire to share abundance with people I love."

Adah put her arm around my shoulders. "Yes, I do understand you. I hope you will understand us." Her arm felt good, loving, and familiar. Her words felt like a chastisement.

"I will ponder it," I said, not knowing what to think or feel. I squeezed her hand resting on my shoulder. She squeezed back, and the conversation ended. I knew I was failing to see something important, but I was satisfied that I had let them know my intentions and they had told me theirs.

Our love was strong, but my questions were not answered to a point of comfort for me. I would have to carry the words in my heart until they gained meaning for me.

We sojourned two days with my friends, laughing and crying as we recalled some of the events and mischief of our past. Strangely, happy memories seemed just as likely to evoke tears as did the sad ones. Remembering Jarna, for example, left Adah and me with a sense of deep heaviness. Sophronia and Sergius, as they had previously, seemed comfortable, joining in our laughter, sometimes tightening their foreheads in confusion, and appearing sad for Jarna's story.

It was clear, however, once we were heading home, that Sophronia could hardly contain her eagerness to see Timon. I longed a little for the times when Job and I were first married and my days were filled with such constant "figs and pomegranates and special cheeses" love. I determined to set Job and myself to work implementing Sophronia's dreams.

And so began a period of calm, peaceful joy and gratitude for the gifts God had given us. Timon and Sophronia were married in a beautiful ceremony, in many ways like the one Job and I had enjoyed. The feast was lavish as their clothes were fine. In fact, no effort was spared to make the celebration of their union worthy of royalty, which they almost were, being so closely connected to Job.

Over the years, Sophronia gave birth to many beautiful children who, as they grew older, were taught by the same tutors from whom our children learned. I gave birth to four more healthy children as I continued to enjoy my functions as Job's wife.

Job's responsibilities as a leader were multiplying, as were the number of our servants. He was now completely devoted to the daily teaching and study of the Holy Writings when he was not involved in major functions for the Council of Elders. Sophronia and Timon became honored officers trusted with primary care of our wealth. Sergius also became a major functionary, having responsibility for carrying out my plans for charitable distribution of our wealth. In that role, he traveled widely, surveying the needs of our community.

My visits to Adah continued to be regular, though she never did sojourn with me, not even when I gave birth.

Much to my satisfaction, I found time to spend dyeing and weaving, mostly for clothing for our household, but sometimes for gifts to townspeople or others in need.

Job never failed to honor God with sacrifices of the purest of our flock, especially on important occasions. He never failed, either, to show his love for me. True, it was mostly "potage" love, inspired only occasionally by the old excitement.

By the time I was twenty-nine years old, I had given birth to ten healthy children, the last two being daughters. In all, our family was blessed with seven sons and three daughters. My birthing was done.

Both Job and I were happy with the size of our family, and in the tradition of our God, I had the final say about when we would demonstrate our mutual love. With God's blessing, we were able to enjoy each other as husband and wife while avoiding further pregnancies.

Nothing was lacking in our lives: joy in our family, abundant wealth, wide opportunities to practice hospitality and charity, esteem beyond what we had ever anticipated, confidence in God's loving care for us, and the pleasure of devoted friends and servants.

Even our parents were granted long and healthy lives. It was clear that God was rewarding Job richly for his devotion.

Our two youngest daughters had enjoyed betrothal ceremonies that pleased both them and us.

As they approached womanhood, they led lives somewhat similar to what mine had been, and yet different. Each one had a best friendship, just as I had with Adah, but the tribal atmosphere was not at all the same. Our daughters never swept the floor of a tent, or even lived in one. When they helped to mill flour, it was not a necessity, but a fun thing to do when they were spending time with the servants.

They took their meals reclined around our elaborate table with its bronze decorations, not sitting cross-legged around the family pot. They never had the grown-up feeling I had enjoyed of fetching water from the well for the family. A trip to the market was a quick walk in the city, not the expedition Adah and I had enjoyed.

But they giggled with their friends, played at being married and having children, and admired silks, jewelry, and precious oils, which they were not often allowed to buy. Their lessons continued in formal sittings with their teacher, unlike the practical following-along that trained Adah and me. Visits from important members of the Council of Elders were no more exciting than daily chores for them.

And they were given daily chores. We would have failed in their upbringing if we had not required them to be useful wherever they could.

I was particularly pleased with the passion they each brought to carding, dyeing, spinning, and weaving. They were ready to maintain the family reputation.

Life was different for Job and me and our family from the tribal atmosphere in which we had grown up. Almost without realizing it, we had arrived at a pinnacle of life that neither of us had anticipated, planned for, or even dreamed of. It just seemed to happen.

Our married children had established their own households, some in our city and others, like Primus, at some distance from us. All were busy with their own growing families.

That is what we were discussing one day as we sat together enjoying the beauty of our home, the land around us, and the city below.

Our married children and their families were all at the home of Primus, feasting together as they did once each year. We had even allowed our two youngest daughters to travel in the company of a servant to join them in their festivities.

This was a particularly important event, not only because all our offspring would be together, but also because we rejoiced in the fact they all got on so well with each other.

God had truly blessed us in the health and solidarity of our family.

Job, praying for the safety of our whole family, especially that they would remain pious and faithful to God's commandments while they were together, had asked me to arrange to set aside one of the healthiest and fattest calves for the sacrifice he would make when they all came to us after the celebrating was over.

That is what he always did. Being the master of the household, indeed of his whole family, no matter how scattered, it was his responsibility to keep them all practicing the faith with devotion. Ever mindful that it is easy to stray, and especially that his oldest children had not been brought up in the laws of the faith from the beginning, he feared they might offend God in their hearts, or even carelessly commit outright sin.

We were in the early evening of our lives, enjoying the blessings God had bestowed on us, appreciating how much we owed Him in the way of devotion.

In fact, we were just feeling calm, good, and happy as we quietly celebrated our lives together. Seated in the silver-hued, gold-leaf-decorated carved acacia wood chairs our servants had placed for us on the courtyard in front of our home, we looked out over our city, warmed in our hearts and souls by the silver light glistening off the acacia trees, the variegated greens of the sycamores, and the pinks, yellows, reds, and blues of our massive cultivated gardens, rising on the steep terraced hillock approaching our home and the gleaming altar above it. Even our purple garments added to the display, and to the awareness of God's gift to us of great good fortune.

Below us in the city moved the occasional group of camels inside our city wall, and the constant comings and goings of our servants, their families, and their animals, wandering through the lush display of their own private gardens.

Everyone in the city had, over time, adopted our God as their own, perhaps because they witnessed the blessings Job and I received, or perhaps because they recognized themselves as fortunate, or perhaps because worship of God just felt good to them. Whatever the reason, the men were dedicated enough to have submitted to the required circumcision, and all were devoted to following the laws as Job taught them.

We were alone together as we had been on the first day after our wedding celebrants had left us, but certainly not lonely as we viewed the fruits of our lives together. The sun was in its quiet season, surrounding us with warmth, but calmly, without the searing waves of truly hot summer. I thought of the contrast between this day and those of my frantic journey with Nefer in my belly, in search of Job's god. What a mistake I might have made had I not accepted our God. I reached out to touch Job and felt a sweet twinge of figs and pomegranates.

11

The Trials

In an instant, it was over. It began when the action in the city below us turned into a rustle of confused activity. The chill in my body told me before anything else that this was no ordinary event. Job's alerted posture testified to his feeling the same way. As if we were yoked together, we were on our feet at the same time, straining to assess the action more clearly. Then we saw our servant Zosimus staggering toward us in the distance.

"Master, the Sabeans attacked us while the oxen were plowing and the donkeys were grazing. They took them all, and killed all the servants tending them. They left only me alive to come and tell you."

Shuddering almost beyond control, my body reproduced my awful childhood fears of cruel and destructive people. They had been vague fears of what might happen; now the horror was happening right before our eyes.

I have to make my body firm. So many deaths. We must arrange for the burials. Who will console their families? How will we ever make up for the loss of all these animals?

Sinking back into my chair, I was about to tell Zosimus to go refresh himself in whatever way he required when the wild atmosphere below us drew our eyes to our servant Tacitus running and falling in a desperate effort to reach us. He fell down beside Zosimus, trembling uncontrollably, able only to scream silently at first.

I glanced at Job, ashen and silent as I was. I was not shuddering now, nor was my body firm. I was without feeling even as I smothered more pain than had ever before filled me.

Then Tacitus spoke. "Lightning struck from the sky and destroyed all the sheep and the shepherd boys. I am the only one who survived it and I rushed to tell you."

I could not move. I was a stone monument affixed to my seat. Neither Job nor I could speak to tell these poor servants to care for themselves. I tried to reassure myself. *We were happy in our early years, without our great wealth. We can survive this loss. We are still alive. Our family is still alive. I must not think of myself, for I have to attend to the poor people whose loved ones died in these attacks.* A painful numbness was growing inside me as if more pain was coming. The strain in my legs made me aware that I was half rising from my seat, my back stiff and my neck tight. *All those lives lost. And only a few moments earlier, we had been celebrating our lives so calmly. We were so sure we lived under the protection of God. Where is God now?*

My thoughts were ripped away when the scene below us seemed to undulate in random confusion like a huge slithering snake and we saw a third servant weaving, falling, and crawling his way up to us like an agonized spirit hardly connected to his own body.

The day became a dream, a nightmare. The trees and flowers and camels sank into the earth. The families we had been watching vanished. Everything around us had disappeared into emptiness, except for this servant approaching the fetid remains of our lives.

Falling on top of the other two messengers, he managed to say, "Chaldeans have attacked. They took the camels, killed the boys tending to them, and ran off. I barely escaped to bring you news."

Thought was impossible. Movement was impossible. I do not know what Job was thinking. Like me, he was without words.

And then it happened, that which could never be, that which was too insufferable to survive. I knew it when I saw the wild-eyed approach of the servant who had escorted our youngest daughters to the home of Primus. I knew even before he was able to gather his breath and form the words.

"A tornado came out of the desert and struck the house of Primus, pulling the walls of the house down on your family. Dead. They are all dead. All dead." He came apart in uncontrolled sobbing.

I think the other servants just looked on in horrified silence. I am not sure. Everything blurred and clouded over. Job fell up out of his seat, staggered up to the altar, tearing his clothes off as he went, and fell facedown in the ashes. The altar had lost all color. The whole world and the heavens had turned to sickly green, ashen death.

I forced myself to leave my writhing agony behind me. There I left all feeling as I called for Timon.

"Quickly gather all the linens you can find that can be used for burial. Take my clothes; take whatever I have woven, whatever anyone else can find. Here, I am ripping these loose sleeves from my tunic. Take them. They are symbols of a dead life. Choose some of the household servants to accompany you to the home of Primus and begin burying the dead. We cannot leave their bodies to decay without respectful care. I will send for more help for you."

Sergius and Sophronia were already near me, speechless, ashen, and trembling. Timon embraced Sophronia quickly and hurried off. "Sergius," I directed, "go to Ruel. Tell him what has happened and ask him to send word to Uncle Eliphaz. I am sure Ruel will want to go help Timon bury the family. Maybe my mother-in-law will be strong enough to travel here to give comfort."

"Sophronia, there is no time to cry. Go first to my family, tell them what has happened. They will come to help. Then go to Adah and let her know I need her comfort."

I turned to Zosimus and Tacitus. "Do what you can to refresh yourselves, take what you need for supplies, and go in search of any stray animals who might have escaped."

They staggered off, and my body returned to the writhing agony I had left behind me.

My precious children. My Primus, your birth as fresh as if it happened yesterday. My first daughter, your sweet mouth on my breasts. My two youngest, here with us only yesterday. Dear Nefer, delivered with such love into Job's hands. All my children—so loved, loving, respectful, and blessed with good health. All our dear servants, gone. Job, so handsome, strong, pious, and respected. Job, I need to be with you.

I think I did not have the strength to walk. I guess I crawled to join Job in the ashes. Poor Job, his whole purpose focused on worshiping and praising God. Was it less than an hour ago that we were thanking God for all his blessings? Was it less than an hour ago that we believed God was fair and just? I lay next to my husband as well as I could, but my agony kept me writhing in pain and anger.

"Job, Job, my dear Job, how could your god do this to us? No one has been more dedicated, worshipful, and law-abiding than you."

I was too shocked and exhausted to stand, yet I could not stay still. "Job, my dear Job. I cannot bear to see you unclothed. Let me send for someone to find a robe for you. Job..."

I had no desire to touch him, nor did he reach out to me. There was no way either of us would be comforted.

As I faded in and out of the world, I ached at the sight of my Job naked. With each lucid moment, I begged him to allow me to find coverings for him, but he made no response, and I had no will to raise myself from the ashes and act without his desiring it. The day darkened and turned again to light before I felt enough to know my anger. "Job, how could your god do this to you?" Job's answer came from the depths of his despair, like an animal's empty, tortured groan.

"Dara, I was born naked; I will die naked. What the Lord has given, he has taken away. Blessed be his name."

With whatever feeble energy I could dig out of myself, I was angry at his acceptance, and at his god. Uncle Ruel had sold me the idea that Job's god was just! My heart ached at the sight of Job's suffering. I had lost everything, but he had lost his god's favor, the one thing that had ruled his life for so long now. I had lost everything, and he had lost more.

I lay with him throughout the day, but we could give each other no comfort. When I reached out to touch him, I felt agitated stillness like the throes of an animal finally yielding to death. Despair pored out of his inert body. And, as my mother had predicted long ago, my body felt at one with his – a feeling I resisted.

Townspeople had begun to gather, many to stare in curiosity and to mock. How eagerly some people take joy in the fall of a great man. Young people especially gathered to ridicule his nakedness as he lay in the ashes. Job begged for all to leave him alone. No one could fully understand or share his grief, not even I. He wanted to be alone with his god, I think.

Some of our most faithful servants gathered silently nearby holding watch over us though they were clearly uncomfortable. It reminded me of the trouble Sophronia and Timon had sitting with the rest of us at Adah's. A breakdown in the space between master and servant can be unspeakably painful, even humiliating. The servants felt the mortification of the fall of their leader more than they could stand to watch.

No matter how deep my own grief, I could not suffer watching Job in his agony. Finally, raising myself up, I brushed the ashes off my sleeves and arose, gesturing to the servants gathered there. Two of the men responded, walking hesitantly toward me. "Please," I said, "erect a tent around him. At least we can protect your master from the cruel laughter of those who come to mock." They departed more quickly than they had approached, happy, I think, to have something useful to do.

Once I was standing, I realized how long I had maintained the same position next to Job. Shaking off more of the ashes, I began to move slowly, this time for the sake of my own body and to search for the sackcloth I believed Job would be willing to wear.

When I brought the covering to him, he sat up slowly and painfully in order to don the clothing. I realized as he did so that his pain was now more than just the agony of loss. His body was beginning to torment him as well. But he resisted the cup of water I encouraged him to drink, allowing me only to dip my fingers in it and wet his lips.

My emergence from the ashes increased my awareness of the mood of the community. Grief, dismay, anger, and some disdain pervaded the city. After all, most had built their faith on the justice and fairness of Job's god. Certainly what had happened was not fair. I heard some of them worrying they would also be mistreated by Job's god just as he had been.

I think Astarte was removed from hiding in a number of homes. Indeed, I had thought to return to Astarte, wondering whether these disasters were her punishment for abandoning her.

Others did not lose their faith in the justice of Job's god, but instead began to search for ways in which Job deserved this disaster. Many, whatever they were thinking and feeling, brought food to our servants to provide for us, along with offers to make a gift of one of their animals. Only a few spoke to us directly, and then with eyes averted and mouths tremblingly distorted. All were speechless and impotent as they tried to grapple with the truth of our family's destruction.

I thought the comfort of loved ones around me would restore me, but time passed before anyone was able to arrive. The continued presence of faithful townspeople provided some warmth and comfort, just as the mockers caused sadness and dismay. But my eyes frequently wandered toward the city gate, looking for the arrival of familiar loved ones.

In the meantime, the focus of whatever strength I had left was entirely on Job, who refused to eat. I understood that. I had no desire for food either, but I forced myself to take water and milk and some flat bread. I joined him frequently where he had raised himself to a sitting position in the ashes inside his tent, begging him to accept the bread and cheese I brought to him. But he refused everything except a few drops of water.

In the midst of attending to Job, I was assaulted by images of my children, sometimes laughing, sometimes crying, sometimes just being present, and sometimes lying distorted in death. I shut those visions away immediately, only to have them pierce my awareness again. The smiling images were just as painful as the death scenes.

I became more and more distraught, frantically seeking to do something. There was no dirt floor of a tent to sweep and carding wool helped only for a few minutes. There was no one to tell my anguish to. I found the basket with my doll and Astarte. I tried holding each of them in turn. There was no comfort there.

Eventually, helpers did begin to arrive. I had lost all sense of time's passage, but at some point many of my sisters and brothers came, with their families and gifts of food. Several of them had gone out first to see whether they could help to round up some animals that might have escaped the raiders and the lightning. They had little success, but, as they pointed out, the way of sheep and goats is that a few will, in time, become many.

Zosimus and Tacitus returned with similar news, and with the same hope that those they had found would multiply. They were exhausted but, I think, relieved they had been able to do something helpful. I knew also that they would now allow themselves the time to relive the horror and to mourn. It was important to leave them alone.

With the arrival of my family, I felt I was reaping some of the results of my own actions when I had temporarily overcome my own shock and grief to dispatch the servants. It was like sitting once again in the V of my father's lap, or settling into the comfort of my mother's conversation when I was emerging into young adulthood. As if there were still something real and ordinary in life. But my body knew the constant pain of a life totally bereft of hope.

Still, I longed especially for the return of Timon. Some unreal part of me hoped this had all been a bad dream and I imagined Timon might come back with a smile on his face. One look at him when he returned and I knew I could no longer deny the reality that I would never see any of my children again.

Now I ached to hear details of their death and burial. How and where had he found them? How did they look? In what linens or other weavings had he buried them? Had

Ruel's family arrived to help?

Poor Timon, what a terrible task. He had been nauseous when he found them, and almost fell ill again in telling me. But he did give me the details, awful as they were. He seemed to understand that I needed to know them. I nursed the information over and over again, and shared it with Job who listened speechlessly. I knew that Timon would never be the same again after this experience.

And yes, Uncle Ruel had been there to help. Poor Uncle Ruel. What terrible grief. He arrived some time later, having returned home to fetch my mother-in-law. We all sat in silent support. No words would help. I thought being together would ease the grief, but the first ray of hope quickly faded. Nothing could relieve the agony except for total numbness.

I surged back and forth between excruciating pain and alarming emptiness.

Tragedy, however, sometimes brings surprises. One was a visit from Jarna. She arrived alone and embraced me silently. I was strangely comforted. For a long time we spoke no words, until she told me, "I had to come to you in your time of troubles. You were such a help to me in mine."

My thoughts leapt back to the acacia tree under which we had sat together, trying to find some good in the terrible fact of her betrothal to an old man with several wives. But I hardly heard anything else she had to say. Just her presence was a gift. Later, I was able to remember her telling me she did indeed have a comfortable life, as my mother predicted, and had given birth to many healthy children who were devoted to her. She even described what my mother had called a "potage love" that had developed for her husband.

I was not able to absorb the meaning of her message then, but later I could remember that sometimes good comes out of the most terrible horror. It had for Jarna.

I waited now only for the arrival of Sophronia with Adah. I could see that Timon also was painfully anxious to see his wife. She did arrive some time after his return, with my mother and father. Their journey had been hard as they had both developed some pain in their bodies.

But Adah was not with them.

"Adah fell to her knees in tears, but she refused to come."

I made Sophronia repeat it.

"Adah refused to come."

I had thought I was beginning to regain some strength, but my insides collapsed when I heard this news. "Why? Did you explain to her what had happened, how I needed her?"

"I begged her. She just said she could not come."

I do not remember how I got there, but I found myself alone in the women's room, staggering from one wall to another, dropping to my knees then rising to pace unsteadily. *"Adah, Adah, Adah. Why? Why, Adah?*

The tears I had contained for so long spilled in noisy eruption. I fell to the floor in exhaustion.

I do not know how much time had passed as I awoke, groaning. Adjusting my wet clothing, I returned to the altar, to Job's tent in the ashes. I did not see Adah again until the end of our lives approached.

I did, however, have the unexpected blessing of Jarna's visit, and I was now surrounded by family and tribe. I had community again, the kind I had thrived on in my growing-up years. Nothing could relieve my agony, but it was shared with others.

Day and night became one for me, I knew not how much time had elapsed.

Job's sadness grew deeper, his remoteness more complete. His flesh was growing yellow, hanging loose on his body. His muscles sagged. He was consuming his own flesh from the inside. As time passed, he was more accepting of my sitting with him, only, I think, because he remained unaware of anything going on around him.

To tell the truth, I was beginning to get a little exasperated. I did not have the strength to have one of my outbursts, but I was erupting internally. I needed Job to be with me in our shared suffering.

If I can force myself to eat, why can he not? After all, I have lost all my beloved children. Nothing could be worse than that. And I am the one who gave birth to them. Does he think he is the only one suffering? I cannot stand to see Job like this. My friend, my strength is putrefying before my eyes.

But I did not give up. "You must eat. You are decaying inside, and the smell of your breath is terrible."

Still he was obstinate, refusing to eat and accepting water only in small drops. I told myself it was that same tenaciousness that sustained him in his refusal to give up on his god, even though he had been treated so unfairly. Indeed, it was his firm belief in the power of his god that kept him alive even as he suffered such despair.

It was my own unyielding concern for Job, I think, and maybe even anger, that kept me from falling further into lonely desolation.

When he developed terrible boils all over his body, from head to toe, I redoubled my effort to get him to eat, and even to bathe. Clearly starvation and ashes were ending his life. The purpose of my life was ending too.

What little hope I had managed to recapture when my family arrived was spent.

Job just sat there scratching his boils with broken pieces of pottery. It was intolerable.

I had nothing left. Even my love for Job was fruitless

and unreturned, causing me only unbearable pain in my shared feeling with him. Nothing could relieve the anguish.

More and more I repeated to myself something my mother had said long ago.

"You will see. Eventually his happiness will be yours and his pain will be yours. An attack on his body will be an attack on yours and whenever he is spared, you will be spared. And he will know you in the same way."

It became clearer and clearer. The only resolution was to die. But I could die only with Job. And he was in no condition even to consider the possibility of allowing death to end his torment. It seemed to me he had gone beyond the point where he was even thinking.

Finally, in my hopelessness, I knew what I had to do for the sake of both of us. Daily I had been joining him in the ashes, for the most part wordlessly. This time, though, I tore my own clothes into rags and covered myself from head to toe with the burnt ruins of his previous offerings to his god. This day I broke the silence.

"How long will you go on with this uprightness? Why won't you admit that your god has abused you for no just cause? Curse your god and die."

Then I will also die, and this pain will end.

Job stared at me with light and life in his eyes that I had not seen since the day the trials began. The husband who had looked at me with such fiery urgency so many years ago boiled up from the depths of his soul as I evoked and challenged the very source of his power. He seemed to come alive with dismay and disbelief and I began to tremble in awful anticipation. Fear crawled through me as I watched him straining to overcome his lethargy in an effort to make sense of my words, and the fact that I had said them.

Eventually he spoke with a clarity I had not heard from

him since he had collapsed into the ashes. "Dara, I would have expected better from you. Now you are sounding like any ordinary foolish woman. We had no trouble accepting good fortune from God. Only a short time ago we were thanking Him for that. Surely now we can accept the bad fortune, too."

I felt myself growing smaller and withering as I dissolved into tears. I think it was terrible guilt and awful disappointment.

But there was hope there, too. Job had come back to life, if ever so briefly. His look embraced me as he watched my tears. It was so much like the look he gave me when I rode off with Sophronia and Timon and Sergius so many years ago in my search for peace after he challenged me to give up Astarte.

So, we would not die. My tears subsided. Strangely, I felt relieved. Though Job had clearly chastised me and, even worse, was disappointed in me, I felt his closeness and love again. Maybe it was seeing his energy. Maybe it was that old feeling of the power of his faith. Maybe it was being caught short in my own selfishness. For whatever reason, I felt better. The distance that had seemed to be growing between us collapsed. Separate agony became shared suffering.

His eyes followed me as I walked away from him, a little taller than I had been when I joined him in rags and ashes. I kept his eyes with me throughout the rest of the day.

Job, refusing to return to the house, remained inconsolable. The only movement he made was occasionally to emerge to sit in the ashes outside the tent I had ordered raised for him and to accept a sip of water. Then he would return to lie secluded in his tent.

Just as Job had torn off his clothes, I had torn away any

inner consolation with which I might have clothed myself. I could not help my Job whose body was decaying as if he were in his grave.

I remembered with awful sadness the look of love, infused with fiery power and determination, that I had sensed in him when he told me to get rid of Astarte, and briefly again when he chastised me in the pile of ashes. I would give away the house and servants who remained just to see that look again, to suffer that terrible argument, even to feel the pain of my frantic search for Job's god.

His god had been the center of Job's life and, as the patriarch of the family, his almost total responsibility. Just as I had offered the maintenance of our daily lives and wealth as a gift to him, so he had given our family and me the blessing of sacred wealth. No one could have been more pious. Once he had dedicated himself to his one god, he had never questioned his choice, never doubted his god's power, never strayed from his belief.

No one's life had been so righteous and no one was angrier than I as I watched the suffering he was enduring. The center of his life had betrayed him. There was no possibility that I could even begin to fill that emptiness. I was beginning to fear that Job's god did not even exist, at least not that god of justice Uncle Ruel had talked about. I think maybe Uncle Ruel was beginning to doubt too.

12

The Comforters

I had grown accustomed to the comfort of my family main-taining presence and help in the background, careful not to intrude on the delicate balance of my feelings. The time came, however, when some of them had to return to their own lives. I understood that. Terrible as our fate was, they had their own responsibilities to tend to. I knew they were ready to return should I call for them again, and truly even their presence had not reduced my anguish. Nothing could.

My parents, however, remained. So did Uncle Ruel and my mother-in-law, having reached the stage in life where their flocks were well cared for by others, and their presence was more important here with their suffering son. I had not, however, anticipated what would happen as I saw the rest of my family depart the city gate. Suddenly my body suffered such agony that I could not stand. As I fell to the ground, weeping in great loud gasps, my parents and in-laws gathered around me, seeking in despair for a way to help.

"No, no, do not try to stop me. Do not try to comfort me. Do not try to lift me to my feet. Do not watch. Please go to Job. I need to be alone."

Oh God. Oh Astarte. Oh Job, where is your god now? Where is my comfort? Let me die. Let me die.

I know not how long I lay on the ground. My parents and in-laws had honored my request. I was alone with my grief, like sharp claws scratching at my insides. Several times I tried to stand, only to be thrown to the ground by my pain. The sky was beginning to change into its evening colors when finally I was able to pull myself into a sitting position. And there I remained, watching the gray of my vision blend with the darkening of the sky.

Finally, I was able to rise and move slowly and achingly toward the ashen altar. I had gone only a short distance when I encountered Sophronia waiting for me. She had, apparently, been standing guard at a distance.

Poor Sophronia, how she did suffer my loss with me. As she had so often during these terrible days, she walked with her arm around me, encouraging whatever peace and strength I had left in me.

As I approached Job I noticed a bent old man standing nearby. In shock, I realized it was Uncle Ruel. Again my tears flowed. Sophronia tightened her hold on me, for which I was grateful. I feared I would sink to the ground again. My strong, powerful, confident father-in-law was gone.

Nothing is left to me. Even those who are living are dead.

Poor Uncle Ruel. During this time of terrible mourning, I had watched him becoming more bent, wizened, and gray, even as my mother-in-law seemed to grow smaller and smaller. Job and I had lost all our children to sudden death, but maybe it was even worse for Ruel and Beta to witness this slow decay of their once handsome and powerful son.

All of us who loved Job seemed to understand the importance of letting him suffer alone without having to worry about the effect it was having on us. So the days continued in an unhappy ritual of trying to eat, trying to rest, and wandering without purpose.

I was grateful that Sophronia stayed by my side, taking on my responsibilities to provide food and care to those who remained.

Then came hope. As I was returning from another futile effort to get Job to take food, I felt him stirring behind me.

His body had straightened as his eyes fixed on something in the distance. It was Uncle Eliphaz, approaching with his friends Bildad and Zophar. As they came closer, my eyes discerned a path opening up in which the trees and flowers seemed to emerge in their full colors. Their camels shone gold and silver in the reflected brightness of the sun and my anticipation, heightened by the red, yellow, blue, and orange of their coverings.

As they approached the city gate, they seemed to gain such stature that I almost fell to my knees at the regal sight. Swaying tall and graceful on their mounts, they carried a message of life and strength.

Surely their presence will be Job's salvation. This visit by his powerful equals will comfort him. They will help restore Job's knowledge that he is still an important and valued leader.

But as they approached close enough to see Job, naked but for the sackcloth, my vision of their great size diminished. In shocking unison, they dismounted and began a slow, almost dirge-like approach, seeming to stumble in disarray as they moved close enough to discern the sores and scabs on Job's emaciated body.

The colors I saw around them faded to a dismal gray. In a display of shared grief, they began tearing their own clothes, a powerful demonstration of their respect and sympathy.

Reaching Job in the ashes, they sank cross-legged around him, maintaining silence as is appropriate for those in mourning. Even as I presented the wine and refreshment provided by Sophronia, no words were spoken. Job, mindful of his responsibility as a host, dipped a piece of bread in the wine and ate it, as if in a ritual, a gesture which did not, however, presage an increase in his ability to take sustenance.

Perhaps it was only my hope creating an image I wanted

to see, but Job's eyes did seem brighter in the presence of these exalted guests.

After I served them, it seemed important to leave these men alone in the healing circle they had formed, so I seated myself on a hillock at some distance from the ashes. From this position I could hear their words—if they were to speak any—without seeming to intrude. As had become her custom, Sophronia settled down beside me, placing her hand briefly on mine.

Uncle Ruel and Aunt Beta wandered back and forth from our hillock to wherever their feet took them, searching as I was for something to still the agony inside.

How hard it must be for Ruel, once an important figure in this group and now simply the observing, grieving father.

"Surely these men will help your husband to recover his strength. Even in his torn clothing, Master Eliphaz fills the area around him with a sense of his royal power. Bildad attends to him as if his every expression were a command, while Zophar seems to lean forth in careful attention to every gesture he makes. I feel honored to be so close to their presence."

"I too hope, Sophronia, that good will come from their presence. Their quiet joining in his grief is a testimony to the high esteem in which they hold him."

Again, Sophronia touched my hand as if to offer the same respect to me in my suffering.

In this manner, in silence, the day passed into evening.

"Sophronia, I will go now to offer them quarters in our home. We cannot have our guests abiding in the ashes, exposed as my Job has chosen to be."

And so I approached them, offering a safe resting place, but Eliphaz spoke for the first time, not with words, but with a firm gesture of dismissal, pushing his palms toward me as if to turn the offer back unaccepted.

Returning to Sophronia, I asked her to request some of the servants to erect a tent near the altar to which the men might repair for the night. When she returned, she carried with her an evening repast of which Job's guests were happy to partake. Then, as darkness settled, they quietly repaired to their tent, emerging in the morning to continue their watch.

In this manner, Eliphaz, Bildad, and Zophar spent a week keeping silent vigil with Job, while Sophronia and I observed from our distant hillock.

Oh, what hope I had placed in the arrival of Eliphaz and his friends. What vain hope it was! I do not know what held me there, watching from afar, observing nothing but stillness with an occasional shifting of position. In truth, it was only my unwillingness to move. Occasionally my parents joined us. They too were wandering as if lost in some strange place that evoked no interest.

Somewhere around the third day I saw Elihu come riding in. Dismounting at the altar, he did not tear his clothes in sympathy as he sat with the group.

What is he doing here? Does he offer hope? I think not. He seems not to grasp the immensity of what has happened.

Indeed, Elihu's presence seemed to make no change in the gathering around the ashes of the altar. Things just went on as if he had not come, though Sophronia did assure there was enough additional food to provide for him as well.

It was on the seventh day of the vigil, as we were all together, watching in silence, that I heard Job's voice. Thin and weak, but unfaltering, his words whispered as if sifted through blowing sand.

I cannot be sure how much was actually spoken, or what was my imagination as I tried to make sense of the lament I was hearing. The lament was long, but only a few words were clear to me.

"Curse the day I was born," he said.

I know what you mean, I thought. Had I not proposed death as an escape from the anguish?

As if our thoughts were joined, Job continued, "Why did I not die at birth? Then I would be at rest. Why can I not join those happy ones who have been relieved from their groaning, rejoicing in the grave."

I grasped Sophronia's hand. "Do you hear him? Do I understand him well? Is he pleading for death?"

"I believe so," she whispered, her voice stopped by her tears. I saw Uncle Ruel nodding, his face ashen except for a touch of inflamed red on his cheeks.

Oh Job, how I share this desire with you. And it is all so much worse because we knew the joy of such blessings. If we had never had the family and the status and the wealth and the faith, we would never have known the pain of losing everything.

I know he continued his lament even as his voice faded. I could no longer hear the words. But words were not necessary. My Job was so bereaved he could find no good except to end the pain by death.

And yet, I was at the same time encouraged because those days of terrible despairing silence seemed to be ended, as if he were coming back to life even as he wished he had never been given life.

Then Eliphaz spoke, his voice strong, commanding, and confident, directing a long speech to my husband. This is the message I heard. "Job, you have instructed so many people, guiding them when they stumbled along the way. You know those who do wrong will be chastised. Can you not see that you also have to accept chastisement for your wrongdoing?"

I had felt better when Eliphaz began to speak, but my

relief quickly changed to anger.

No, my Job has been painstaking and constant in his worship of his god. Don't even suggest that he—and I—deserved these terrible losses.

I felt Job's parents stiffening behind me, feeling, I believe, the way I did.

This is no way to comfort a man suffering as deeply as Job is. This is not comfort, this is a cruel, heartless, ignorant attack.

Eliphaz had just told Job to stop complaining and accept his punishment; he had accused my husband of wickedness. Eliphaz—the wise elder who had helped Job to find his way to his god, who had helped him to his righteous life—was accusing him of depraved sinfulness. Job, so very pious and righteous, to be accused of wickedness. It was unthinkable. I longed for the energy to plant myself in front of Eliphaz and thrash him with words.

"How fortunate is the one," Eliphaz continued, "whom God reproves. You should, therefore, not reject the discipline of the Almighty. He punishes, but He also heals." And on and on he went with insufferable failure to recognize the depth of Job's pain.

Behind me I heard Aunt Beta moan, even as I felt Uncle Ruel stiffen further. I could only imagine what he must have been thinking and feeling.

Eliphaz was the respected elder and teacher on whom Ruel's faith relied and now he was uttering what could not be true. "There is no one like Job," Ruel almost shouted. "There is no one like him on the earth, a blameless and upright man who fears God and turns away from evil. Eliphaz is torturing Job with a lie." *Is Ruel having second thoughts about Eliphaz's teaching? I wouldn't blame him.*

Does Eliphaz still believe what he's saying, even after witnessing the horror we have suffered, even after seeing the devastation these terrible events have wrought. Does he really think Job did something so awful that his god would take everything away from him? That his god would really kill all our children and those innocent servants?

I felt a change in my body as power seemed to rise from the bottom of my feet to the top of my head. I leapt to my feet, ready to do something with the anger that was growing. Sophronia was right beside me, holding my elbow as if to restrain me. From what? What did I think I could do?

Apparently it seemed obvious to Eliphaz that God protects the righteous and punishes the sinful. Is that not what Uncle Ruel had taught me? Job's god was a god of justice. As long as we did the right things we would be blessed with good fortune. Therefore, it made sense to Eliphaz that Job must have broken his god's commandments in some terrible way to bring such awful chastisement upon himself.

Job, he advised, should accept that God's discipline was meant to strengthen him, if only he would acknowledge his wickedness. Then he could accept the manifold gifts God would grant him in return.

Eliphaz seemed so satisfied with himself for having found the way out for Job. I tried, with no success, to understand that poor Eliphaz might be going through stress of his own, believing in Job's innocence and yet convinced that God punishes only the wicked.

Is Eliphaz so stuck in his belief that he cannot see the possibility that he might be wrong?

But my Job was not willing to lie by admitting sin that he had not committed. I felt power returning to his voice. "As long as I breathe and the spirit of God is in me, I will not lie. I will not say you are right. Until I die, I will not give up my integrity. I hold fast to my righteousness and I will not let it go. My heart does not reproach me for anything that I have done."

With his words, Job caused my heart to expand. Had I ever felt such pride in him? I think not. In the midst of despair he would not give up either confidence in his own integrity or his faith in his god.

To him, God is real.

There he was, demanding that God give him an explanation. You do not demand answers from a non-existent god. As for me, I longed for an answer for both of us.

I found strength in Job's unwavering belief, but I could not share in it. I was dismayed by this god we had adopted. He was not the god of fairness that Uncle Ruel had sold me on. I knew that because I knew Job. It seemed to me there was no hope for me in any deity. Astarte no longer had any power, and, whether he acknowledged it or not, Job's god had betrayed him. I was desolate.

I was buoyed with pride, though, when Job responded to Eliphaz with honest acceptance of his failings. "True, I am not perfect. No one is. God understands that His creatures are flawed and forgives those imperfections. But as for my being wicked, I will not admit to that lie. Nor will I accept that God is always fair by our human standards. Look at all the times that very wicked people live wonderful, long, wealth-filled lives. God is not as simple, Eliphaz, as you make him out to be."

But Job's response just served to provoke several rounds of accusations of his wickedness, with Zophar and Bildad joining Eliphaz in ever more edgy efforts to beat Job into submission with their words.

In between, Job was becoming a bit sarcastic, thanking them for being so kind in their efforts to comfort him. I could not blame him. They just would not let up. Those seven days of silent sympathy had deteriorated into what seemed to me like stubborn inflexibility as they declared themselves to be the arbiters of God's will.

Now even when Job bewailed his condition, they accused him of ranting. They seemed to have no more willingness to comfort him in his despair. At one point, Bildad even suggested our children might have sinned wickedly, bringing about this punishment. As I listened, that was probably the most hurtful assault of all, having just lost our entire family, and knowing how Job sacrificed regularly for the sake of his children.

Somewhere in the midst of their attack on Job, I noticed that the three had once again attired themselves in their regal robes of purple. What an insult to my husband, still mourning in near nudity.

So superior were they apparently feeling that I suspected they would have abandoned their tents near Job to abide in our home. I did not make the offer.

All three men were increasingly inflexible in their speeches. I tried to believe they had Job's welfare at heart, but I confess it seemed to me that what mattered most to them now was the need to prove their own righteousness. Though Job begged him to do so, Eliphaz even refused to look him in the eye to see his innocence. I had a feeling the look in Job's eye was a lot like the one of fiery power and determination he had given me in our argument about keeping Astarte.

Good for you, Job, I thought, silently cheering him on.

He was suffering terribly, but he was unyielding in his integrity. The same resolution that had helped us make our way through our arguments was now strengthening my husband. He would not yield when he knew he was right. But he was not claiming to be perfect either, not like those three "wise" elders who seemed unable, the more they talked, to see any imperfection in themselves or their convictions. From my point of view, it seemed like my Job was the only one including God in the conversation.

I had not realized the strength spreading through me—almost joy, if such a thing were possible in the midst of the horror. Job's body was weak almost to the point of death, but his spirit was reviving. I felt the same power passing through the group gathered around me. Job was our inspiration as he begged God to forgive whatever he had done wrong, but he refused to call himself wicked.

If this were a meeting of the Council of Elders I think Job would be winning his point. How proud I am of him. I feel strength in the way he is looking directly at his tormentors.

I heard him say, in a voice becoming ever firmer, "What sin God sees in me is between me and my God. It is not up to you to accuse me. You are taking too much on yourselves to think you can talk for God, for we cannot always understand his ways. I for one will not presume to understand them all. He is, after all, the All-Powerful. And I will not yield to your demands that I confess a wickedness that is not mine."

Personally, I was annoyed with that youngster Elihu, who had joined the "consolers" halfway through their stay. I really did not mind too much when he sat there in silence, listening to his elders. I could hardly contain my anger, however, when he piped in toward the end of all this, as if he somehow had more wisdom, or at least more power of persuasion, to add his bit to the pressure on Job. This felt particularly insulting to me. At least the other three men were Job's equals. By this time I was tired of the endless debate. I longed for some kind of action. I suppose I even hoped that Job would call for food and wine. Anything to put an end to what I saw as an obviously fruitless debate.

Little did I know how soon my desires would be fulfilled.

Every once in a while, Job in his desperation had called on God to come to him and explain what justified this terrible punishment. Each time he did that, I could see Uncle Ruel wince. I remembered what he had told me about God not wanting to be seen, so I suppose he feared that this boldness on Job's part would bring down more chastisement. As for me, I could not imagine what worse could happen. Maybe I was not a very good follower of God, but I did appreciate my husband's audacity. There were not many with my Job's courage.

It seemed right to me that Job should eventually take his case directly to God. After one last painful round of argumentative pressure to confess to what he knew to be untrue, he felt free to recite to God the whole history of his life: its long period of goodness, generosity, faithfulness, hospitality, and success as well as the details of his suffering since the trials. Then, as if speaking to a judge in a court of law, he challenged God:

> "Grant me one thing only,
> and I will not hide from your face:
> do not numb me with fear
> or flood my heart with your terror.
> Accuse me—I will respond;
> Or let me speak, and answer me.
> What crime have I committed?
> How have I sinned against you?
> Why do you hide your face as if I were your enemy?"[2]

As one, and without speaking, our group was drawn to the altar where Job and his "comforters" were gathered.

I began to tremble as if the entire world were quaking.

What if his god decided to kill Job? I was terrified I might lose my husband—my last hope, really. And Eliphaz and his friends looked pretty frightened too. Even Elihu, the tag-along.

As I shook, so did the heavens. The center of a terrible whirlwind came directly toward us. The pressure on my body nearly crushed me, alternating with the feeling of being pulled out of myself. The sand stung and blinded us, even as it ripped away at our clothing and tore away at whatever skin was exposed. I knelt close to Uncle Ruel just to avoid being thrown about like a piece of linen, even as the deep green darkness enveloped us. Now I knew we would all die. Job's challenge had provoked God to destroy us all.

But that is not what happened. Instead, a Voice spoke from the whirlwind. No, a Voice thundered from the whirlwind. All of us who heard it fell to the ground, thrust by some otherworldly force.

13

The Voices

"Who is this who deems himself worthy to question me with words that reflect ignorance? Stand up like a man and I will demand testimony from you."

The power of the whirlwind lifted Job to his feet, even as it threw the rest of us trembling to the ground. The ashes of God's altar churned in wild rhythm with the sandstorm swirling in from above the city. The tents broke away and flew out of sight. The camels bawled as I had never heard from any animal while they struggled in vain to maintain their footing. As they were thrown to the ground, their acacia platforms flew into the air, trailing the bright attachments that had signified royalty.

From the city below issued a roar of wailing fear. All around was blinding, stinging darkness, tinged with a deep green that seemed to have a heavy weight of its own. Around Job there opened a clear space—around him only. There he stood with unreal vigor, as if the power of the whirlwind had filled him with other-worldly strength, prepared for whatever chastisement was to come.

I felt the presence of no one but our God in the whirlwind. Grasping at sand for support, which it did not afford, I gave myself up to accepting what was happening and whatever was to come. I had no thought, no words, no expectation. Almost buried in ash and sand I yielded myself up, not to despair, but to openness as if my body were one with the wildness around me.

This was the voice of God! A voice that filled the heavens and struck the earth in a thundering echo that tore through the wildness around us. A presence that vibrated through my body with tremors beyond describing. God was speaking to Job!

"Who are you to challenge me? Where were you when I laid the foundation of the earth? Tell me if you know how I accomplished it. Do you know how I established the bounds of the sea? Did you form the circle of the day with its darkness and light? Have the gates of death been revealed to you? By your wisdom does the hawk soar?"

And so God's voice recited the secrets of creation, life, and death that no human could produce.

Then, challenging Job directly, God commanded, "Shall a faultfinder like you contend with the Almighty? If you would argue with God, you must respond."

Job fell to his knees. "I am of small account. I cannot answer you. I have spoken once but I will go no further."

God was not done. "Answer me like a man. Would you condemn me to justify yourself? Do you have the power of God? Can you create a tempest like this that binds you now?"

And the voice continued to smite Job with words describing all that the Almighty had done in forming the earth and those who inhabit it.

With the power God had given him, Job responded with a clear and yet humbled voice and demeanor, "I know you can do all things. I have uttered things I cannot understand, things too wonderful for me, which I did not know. I had heard of you by the hearing of the ear, but now I see you with my eyes. Therefore, I repent in dust and ashes."

When Job was done speaking, the whirlwind withdrew sufficiently to reveal Eliphaz and his friends in the clearing. The voice continued. "My wrath is kindled against you and your two friends, for you have not spoken of me what is right as my servant Job has. Now, therefore, take seven bulls and seven rams, and go to my servant Job, and offer up for yourselves a burnt offering; and my servant Job shall pray for you, for I will accept his prayer not to deal with you according to your folly, for you have not spoken of me what is right as my servant Job has done."

Eliphaz, Bildad, and Zophar bowed their heads into the ground in shame.

I feared the Almighty might read my thoughts and find them unforgivable, but I could not stop them.

My Job suffered such mistreatment from these men, but now they have been chastised and humiliated by God. I cannot help but feel satisfied.

And the turmoil ceased as suddenly as it had begun. The sand and ashes settled to the ground. The sounds of fearful groaning ceased. We who had been groveling in fear and awe hesitantly sat up and brushed ourselves off. The air softened, turning a pale orange-yellow again, and the heat rose in calm waves around us. Job fell to the ground, too weak to stand.

Eliphaz, Bildad, and Zophar seemed to have lost their height as their posture bent in humiliation and acquiescence to the power of God. With great effort, they rose to their feet. Defeated, they moved toward their camels. Weakly, they prodded them to recover themselves. As if confused by sudden age, they found the damaged acacia platforms and placed them on their mounts. Slowly, they mounted. With blank eyes, they surveyed the disarray they were leaving behind. Riding off on their denuded camels to fulfill God's judgment against them, they were as those conquered in battle.

God never did answer Job's charge, and Job never did yield his integrity. We all knew, however, that we would never again pretend to understand God's justice, and Job humbly admitted as much to his god. Nor would we ever again doubt that we had been visited by God the All-Powerful.

I remained stunned in my kneeling position, emptied of all thought, energy, and intention. It was Uncle Ruel who first rose in youthful height and power, filled with the spirit of God. Embracing Aunt Beta, who had herself regained her fullness of confidence, he guided her carefully and eagerly to the aid of their son. Together, they approached Job.

I watched as Ruel tried to help Job to his feet. Job waved him away, gesturing his inability to move on his own. Reactivating my own senses, I rushed to join them, feeling tall myself, and called for Sergius and Timon, even as Sophronia appeared at my right hand.

"Sophronia, please go before your husband and Sergius and prepare a soft bed for Job in our quarters. Timon, with the help of Sergius, convey my husband gently there. I shall meet you at his bedside."

Nearly carrying him, and with great care, given the lack of flesh on his body and the terrible boils on his flesh, they lay him almost reverently on the bed. I ran ahead to cover it with the very soft linen undergarment I had worn on our wedding day. Tucked away in a special place, it had escaped the gathering of burial cloths on the day of the disasters. Now it would serve to ease the pain of lying on the boils, which seemed to be the only thing that covered the bones of his starved body.

Ruel and Beta, displaying a mixture of relief, elation, awe and caution, followed their son to his bed. Job, gesturing to his father, spoke to him from his weakness. I could not hear his words, but I heard the joy in Uncle Ruel's voice when he agreed to go immediately to the altar to sacrifice the fatted calf that had been set aside to celebrate our children's reunion.

Sergius and Timon, their expressions reflecting respect and awe and colored with concern and sympathy, backed out of the room in respect of Job's position of honor. Sophronia withdrew as well, after providing me with soft cloths, water, and oil.

I was alone with my husband. My body surprised my expectations as it swelled briefly with a "special cheeses and pomegranates love." Bending to his forehead, I caressed the air above him with my lips, sparing him painful touch. His eyes returned a gentle message of love and appreciation.

Then Job yielded willingly to my ministrations. Removing all coverings to ease the pain of touch, I slowly bathed and oiled his body, in much the same way that I would many years later to prepare it for burial.

He did take some beer and a bit of flat bread, but he had been so long without nourishment that his desire for food would increase only very slowly.

For both of us, the exhilaration of the awesome encounter with God stood in sharp contrast to the awful desolation and grief of our loss. I fear that my unceasing tears sometimes stung his open sores as I tended to him. But I was no longer alone in my grief and joy. My Job was alive with me again.

The body takes time to heal, but days of eating, drinking, bathing, and strengthening eventually restored Job to the fully healthy, handsome man he had been before the trials began.

Moreover, victory now shone throughout his body as he stood tall in the awesome awareness that God had presented himself to him.

This was a new Job, blessed with a power beyond any he had known before. Uncle Eliphaz and his companions seemed to recognize it when they returned many days later, chastened and humble with the tribute God had commanded. Attired simply as was appropriate to the humble duty they were performing, they rode in on camels that bore no remnants of the regal colors they had once displayed. I wanted to assume that Uncle Eliphaz and his group had been equally transformed, so they would never again be as self-righteous as they had been.

As Eliphaz, Bildad, and Zophar alit from their mounts, Job greeted each of them with an embrace and a kiss on each cheek. "You are welcome, my friends."

Job is more generous than I would be, but I guess this is the way God would have it, I thought as I greeted them with the dignity appropriate to men of stature.

And Job spoke. "Come. Let us sacrifice the rams and feast together with the whole city. I have prayed for you, and God has accepted my prayer. Now we shall celebrate together."

Even as the crowds were gathering, our families returned with songs of rejoicing, offering sympathy at the same time for all we had suffered. One by one they embraced us, each offering Job a gold ring and a gift of money.

The feasting and rejoicing, with music and dancing, continued for many days.

As for me, I could never doubt again. I had heard the Voice of God. I had received a blessing like no other, thanks to the unyielding faith of my husband.

I knew I would never cease to mourn the family I had lost or lose my love for them, but strangely my grief was infused with the God-given spirit that filled me in the whirlwind.

Our children had enriched the world with their lives, and they had died as we all would. As Job had said, "What the Lord has given, he has taken away; blessed be his name."

Now I understood. What gifts we had enjoyed in the past; what gifts God had bestowed upon us now; what gifts he promised us for the future! They were gifts, not wages for our good works. I had no doubt that Job and I would use those gifts for goodness and justice.

I knew as well, beyond any doubt, that my grief would always lay heavy on my body. Understanding and discerning can help, but the loss of all one's children leaves an empty hole behind that will forever ache with a hunger for their presence.

14

After The Rejoicing

The celebration of God's visit came to a gradual end. The townspeople had returned to their daily lives. Those who had jeered at Job had asked for and received forgiveness. Our families returned to their homes, still grieving with us over our terrible losses, but happy to see the hope for our new prosperity. Uncle Eliphaz and his friends rode off, knowing they were still respected royalty in Job's eyes.

We were filled with thankfulness to our families for the aid they had given us. Most awe-filled was our gratitude for God's blessings. The penitential gifts he had required from Eliphaz and his friends, in addition to those offered by our families, had already started us on the road to recovery of our wealth.

Like the bereaved sitting alone after the comforters have gone, Job and I were left with the shock of grief that had been muted by all the distraction. As the last guest exited the gate, I turned to Job, and he to me. Suddenly our tears flowed as they had not done since the days of loss. Supporting each other as our bodies resisted movement, we forced our way slowly to our private quarters.

There we collapsed together in full expression of our emptiness. I do not know how long we grieved thus, or how long we lay together in silent exhaustion after the sobbing ceased.

Clinging in desperate embrace, we had felt the comfort of each other without seeing each other. As our sobbing subsided, we moved to search each other's face.

My expression probably mirrored Job's. His mouth, no

longer twisted in agony, conveyed an easy gentleness I had not witnessed since he rent his clothes and fell into the ashes on that dreadful day. His eyes, swollen by tears, nevertheless shone clear and bright while his skin had lost its chaotic array of discolored eruptions. Gentle lines of age graced his forehead while the deep crevasses were gone.

I surprised myself with laughter, matched by Job's. We had been released to the love of each other. Job pulled me to him in an embrace that was almost happy. I think we even giggled a little in relief as we dressed ourselves in fresh garments.

Grief and tears would forever be ready to reappear when we were least expecting them. For now, though, we were free to return to something like our lives had been.

Thought returned to the needs of those around us. Our servants had suffered terrible losses of friends and family in the initial killings. Those who had reported the awful events had been direct witnesses to the horror. Imagine poor Timon and his helpers, burying the children they had come to love as their own. My tears flowed again, this time in empathy. And consider Sophronia, maintaining control over her own grief as she cared for me.

In truth, Job and I were beginning a new life together, built on shared horror and loss as well as the amazing blessing of God's visit and our deepened love for each other. But our duties remained the same.

And so we emerged from our private quarters to resume our traditional tasks. Sufficiently restored, I was able to summon Sergius to ride out with me to visit the townsfolk. First, however, I ordered Sophronia and Timon to retreat to their own quarters to be with each other and their children for however long it would take to recover. I knew that for them, as for all of us directly affected by the terrible events that had assaulted us, there could never be complete restoration.

But I knew as well that God's visit had created a new kind of strength and ability to experience confidence and joy.

Sergius had already surveyed the town, so I was filled with heightened fear when he told me, "You will be surprised at the conditions left behind by the whirlwind."

"Can it be worse than what I imagine? I expect to find everything covered in sand and ash in spite of efforts to clean it up. At the very least, there must be piles of unsightly waste. With a tempest that powerful, I imagine dead animals who succumbed, and even children, recently buried. I expect to see houses torn into pieces, and acacia trees uprooted, removing whatever shade there had been. And sadness. There must be terrible grief among the people."

Sergius's expression confused me. Was he smiling? Perhaps even laughing? Had the trials so filled this kindly person with evil that he now took pleasure in other people's pain?

As we neared the lower city, I gasped for air as I inhaled the shock of what I saw. Everything seemed more beautiful than it had been before. Houses and trees not only stood firmly in place, they seemed to glow with joy, if it is appropriate to use that word to describe the atmosphere. An abundance of healthy animals filled their customary spaces. Children shouted playfully in their games. Adults came rushing to me in happy greeting. I knew it could not be, but it was as if they had all lost the signs of toil and aging.

"Sergius, is this God's work? Did the tempest heal rather than destroy? It is almost as if it had never happened, except that things are not as they were. Everything seems to have been cleansed and healed."

Of course Sergius could not explain it any more than I

could, except to acknowledge God's gift.

The effect seems to have comforted even those who lost family in the initial trials. Like me, they were in permanent subdued pain. Like me, they were struck with comforting awe.

There was no need for the dispensing of charity. But my presence did offer empathy and support to those who were bereaved. I believe my own suffering magnified the value of my time sitting silently, or occasionally listening or speaking. There is a healing bond that cannot be fully known by those who do not share in the experience.

God did not restore lives that had been taken, but He did touch the spirit with calm, hope, and the ability to know joy.

As I rode out, so did Job. I watched him exit the city gate, sitting tall and confident on his mount, to resume a role that had been left behind as our wealth accumulated. As in our early marriage, he would offer direct supervision over the care of his flocks.

In truth, he knew his supervision was not necessary. Those tending the animals were skilled and loyal. But he intended for his presence to convey his appreciation and confidence.

Reuniting at the end of the day for our evening repast, we eagerly shared the good news of what we had seen.

"Our flocks are increasing well beyond my hope and expectation," Job said, rejoicing. "All who are tending them are amazed at the rapid increase. I believe my presence is not needed."

Once again my breath sucked in almost with pain, except that it felt good. "Oh Job, that is so like what I saw today." And I reported to him what Sergius and I had seen.

"I believe, Dar', that God is at work continuing the blessing he bestowed in the whirlwind."

I hoped God would not be angry with me for my thought, which I did not share with Job: *Could it be this is God's atonement for the injustice he visited on us?*

And so, we settled into life as it had been before and could never be again.

I knew our way of life had been restored when the day came that Eliphaz and his group rode in to meet with Job in discussion of God's word. Now, however, the Word had offered direct testimony. No longer could they maintain the simple belief that those who followed God's laws without deviation were rewarded and those who did not were punished. God had made his complexity known, so the study seemed often more like worship than the exploration of rules to be followed.

Uncle Eliphaz was in attendance as well for the meetings of the Council of Elders. His humiliation delivered by the voice of God seemed to have the effect of increasing not only his faith, but his respected position on the Council as well. God's visit in the whirlwind was brief, but His presence remained.

One activity, however, was never restored. Never again would Job and I suffer the pain of sitting in our position below the altar, surveying the town. There we had experienced such supreme contentment and there we had learned that everything was lost. There is no pain so great as remembering what joy had been that could never be again.

While I felt a new strength and pride, I never did lose the sense of a huge empty cavern within me where my family had been. Often I would see my dear children in my dreams, only to awaken to the emptiness of their absence.

While I felt the continuing power of God's presence, I never stopped accusing Him for the horrors to which He had exposed us. Always guilt and fear followed on the heels of such thoughts. Then I consoled myself with Job's teaching that only if we have a real faith in God can we let Him know our angry thoughts.

With restored health and strength came a new pleasure in sexual love—not so exciting as in our first marriage, but deeper and, somehow, more spiritual.

Out of that love came the first pregnancy of our new family. Truthfully I was not as joyful as I had been before Primus's birth. I had thought I was done with birthing, and now I was starting over. Each change in my body, each sensation of a heavy internal rock, each cramping of my legs, reminded me of my sweet lost children. It was hard not to think of this little one as an inadequate replacement.

I feared, sometimes with sickening terror, for the future of this baby as I had never done in my previous pregnancies.

The time for the birthing came a little over a year after our trials had ended. Outwardly, it was much the same as for the arrival of our firstborn. My mother was there supporting my back, and my mother-in-law was present to receive this child. Several of my sisters were there as they had been before to ease the pain and help with a swift delivery. And, as the pain seized my abdomen, they were all ready to encourage me to push.

I did. I delivered the firstborn of our second family. Outwardly, it was much the same as for the arrival of our firstborn.

But then the most dreadful happening occurred. Shrieking out of my lungs, from the very belly that had just released our new daughter, came a hemorrhage of amassed pain, a surge of tears, a volcano of blackness, the river of tearful groans never sufficiently spent for my first family, the scream for Primus and all who followed.

Job, breaking the taboo against entering the women's quarters, rushed in, anticipating a scene of violent death. Indeed, the memory of death had visited along with the afterbirth.

Dear God, you cannot take our children without knowing that the mourning will never cease.

I was totally lost in my own personal whirlwind of grief. I realized afterward how torn Job had been between containing my wild emotions with a restraining, comforting embrace,and providing our beautiful new child the gentle holding she deserved. Sharing my wild anguish, he held my arms close to my sides in firm, controlled, mutual agony.

Sophronia was present to clean and swaddle our baby, while Job calmed me sufficiently to see our newborn for the first time. Once I was spent and lying on the bed that had been prepared, Job turned to our new daughter.

"She is beautiful, Dar', calm and peaceful like a dove. Her name is to be Jemimah. Dove. This firstborn of our second family is not a son, but shall receive all the inheritance rights of a male child. That shall be true of all the daughters we may have, for God has shown me the equal value of the feminine, as have you in all you have done to sustain our marriage, our wealth, and our family."

He held her gently, even as he had coddled Nefer so many years before. Then he placed her to my breast, and love for her surged from me even as the early fluid flowed in reaction to her determined, dovelike sucking.

This child was not a replacement for lost children. She was a wonderful little person in her own right. Our love for her was as deep as that for our other children had been, but with a special overtone of awe and fear of this delicate life entrusted to our hands.

There was no dramatic announcement of her birth to

a crowd waiting for the news, but a relieved and happy spreading of the word throughout our new household and, indeed, our whole city.

In all, I birthed a new family of ten children. Two sets of twins helped to build our new family more quickly. True to his word, Job bestowed on our two other daughters names that conveyed their beauty, the second daughter was Keziah, or cinnamon, and the third Heren-happuch, or eye-shadow.

Each received Job's blessing of equal inheritance with our sons. His devotion toward them reminded me of the special place I had enjoyed with my father so many years before, and even of the special affection I had always received from Uncle Ruel.

Job and I took pleasure in a long and blessed new life together, enjoying more wealth and power than we had experienced before.

I want to be clear, however. Our love, though new in many ways, also retained the quality of the old. Neither one of us had given up our stubbornness, though I would prefer now to call it persistence. However we name it, my mother's prediction held. We did have our arguments, and we did refuse to give up on each other and our convictions until we had arrived at a resolution.

I never did lose the perpetual ache for the lost children of our first family. Indeed, each new birthing was accompanied by mourning for the children of our past.

Job and I rarely spoke of our mutual grief, but it was always there, mixed with the potage love, and even with occasional "figs and pomegranates and special cheeses."

Sophronia, Timon, Sergius, and all the other servants who had survived the trials recovered energy and spirit, sustaining them through long and fruitful lives. Never forgetting that we are all created in the image of God, we recognized that we each had a different function in the living of our daily lives, but that our value was equal. Each of them enjoyed in some measure the palatial development of his city that accompanied Job's exalted status.

In time each of our parents departed quietly in blessed, comfortable death, as did Uncle Eliphaz at a great old age. And, in the end, so did my husband. Quietly, with his family by his side, Job fell into the permanent sleep. I think his last words were, "What the Lord has given, he is taking away; blessed be his name."

Or maybe those were my thoughts as his eyes closed and his body passed into permanent repose.

And so I sit here now, in the great hall of the King, mourning the end of my story, for Job is my story. I wish I could say I have such faith in God that I am not sad. But I cannot. The depth of my grief is different from the agony I felt at the time of the trials, but somehow more bottomless. Job's death is my death too.

My reminiscences are done. Once again I am aware that Adah is here in the great hall with me. I have not fallen on my knees with her, but pulled her up to meet my daughter Jemimah. "This is my dearest and oldest friend," I am saying through my tears. "This is Adah."

My life has come full circle. Adah is trying to tell me why she did not come to me during the time of trial. But she does not have to. I know.

"And then," she is saying, "I could not come later, because I had not come then."

I know.

"Adah, I am so grateful that you are here now. I am the one who should be asking your forgiveness. I failed to understand how burdensome my demands on our friendship were for you as the differences in our wealth grew.

"I know now. My gifts and visits felt like condescension and my invitations like a summons. But Adah, our friendship was only sleeping for a while. You have restored it."

Adah and I are both widows, with devoted families in whom to take pride. I want her to come live with me, but I understand that she cannot. She has, however, raised a tent with some of her family on the outskirts of the city. I expect once again to experience the familiarity and comfort of her home. Job is gone. My life is returning to the source.

ADDENDUM
The Story Of The Story

The issue of forgiveness seized my attention in the mid 1980s, at a time when I was still engaged in the psychology of women, my special area of instruction during the last fifteen years of my academic career. An essential aspect of forgiveness is concern for justice. Given that I also have a lay student's interest in the Bible, it probably isn't surprising that I chose to study Biblical justice as reflected in the Book of Job. And it seemed especially appropriate to view the story from the point of view of his wife who suffered the severe losses of the trials along with him. So my interests coalesced in what seemed to me to be a very comfortable and meaningful way.

Applying my psychologist's focus to the study, I found myself annoyed with the somewhat pervasive portrayal of "the patience of Job" as a kind of wimpy, uncomplaining acceptance of any punishment, no matter how unjust. I saw him instead as a pretty strong character, one of the first self-actualizers who knew his own strengths and weaknesses and would not yield to anyone's pressure to lie about himself in order to gain favor. I liked that Job.

My career as an academic had schooled me to examine everything I could about a topic of interest. That isn't bad training if one is working on topics that are already familiar, and if the amount of relevant material is reasonably limited. So I began reading about the Book of Job, and discovering interesting interpretations and speculations. But when I visited the Yale Divinity School Library and saw the huge wall of writings about Job, I realized I'd either have to give up the project or curb my perfectionism. I wasn't a theologian, and previous researchers had been more abundant than I could handle and still maintain my own life and professional activities.

I confess that the dilemma froze my Joban activities, but he was never far out of my thoughts. Then, in 1992, Safire identified Job as "the first dissident,"[3] not that different from my Self-actualizing Job, I thought, and I was fired up again. The perfectionism yielded a little, and I thought maybe I could continue to explore Job for pleasure, not as if I were writing a dissertation.

The Job I liked had a firm commitment to justice rather than self-righteous justification. In 2000, my sister provided me with a book by Alan Dershowitz[4] which helped me understand more clearly the covenant relationship which Job invoked in his demand that God declare the charges he had against him. Like a good lawyer, Job called on his right to know, and the demand was justified with God's appearance to him and the ultimate restoration of his family and wealth. And I felt a little more free to enjoy Job.

Not only was Job a self-actualizing dissident with the courage unyieldingly to maintain his integrity, he was also an early feminist. Why else would such a point be made that he named the three daughters in his second family and saw to it that they got an equal share of the inheritance? To name is to grant power, as is inclusion in one's will, so to speak. Of course, the Biblical story doesn't mention the daughters in his first family. He probably named them too, as he would have done all his children. But the writer of Job chose to make a point of his care for the three daughters in his second family. Something must have happened during the trials or as their consequence to inspire him to act in such a counter-cultural manner. So Job himself opened up the issue of the women in Job's life.

Job's wife is mentioned three times in the Book of Job (NRSV). First, in 2:9-10,

"Then his wife said to him, 'Do you still persist in your integrity? Curse God, and die.' But he said to her, 'You speak as any foolish woman would speak. Shall we receive the good at the hand of God, and not receive the bad?' In all this Job did not sin with his lips."

The most common understanding of this encounter has been, over the centuries, to accuse Mrs. Job of being in league with the devil. That interpretation is a little unsatisfactory, since neither she nor Job knew the exchange that was taking place between God and The Satan, or the Accusing Angel,[5] who, by the way, was then an agent of God and not the Devil we have come to know in later times.[6]

Other explanations include the suggestions that the word for "curse" could also be translated "bless," that Mrs. Job is invoking a customary Jewish usage of the opposite to express the real meaning of her intent, or, in a more humorous vein, cartoons and poems about the nuisance Job is, sitting around in the ashes, while she has to do all the work. ("Lift your legs," she says to the seated Job in one cartoon, while she vacuums under his feet.)

Those of us who study the history and psychology of women are not surprised by the identification of Job's wife with the devil. It has been tradition, until feminist reexamination changed our way of looking at things, to identify women with evil. But that's another fascinating and ongoing study of women in the Bible which can wait for another time.

I have chosen to extract three major points from this encounter, the first of which requires knowing the situation from outside, when God tells The Satan to spare Job's life. In my story, I have chosen to see that Mrs. Job's life was therefore spared since, as Job's wife, she was one with him, a part of him, and therefore covered by the injunction to spare his life.

If you see that as a stretch, I understand why, but two other points seem more obvious to me, and, I think, may be more acceptable to you. His reply to her, essentially saying, "Now you sound like any foolish woman" suggests to me that he holds her in high respect, surprised when she sounds foolish. Like the claim in the previous paragraph, I have chosen to make this respect an integral part of the story of Mrs. Job.

Finally this exchange has provided the opportunity for a clear statement from Job that God is in charge, and may mete out both good and bad. There is nothing in this response that would reflect the views we will hear from his so-called comforters who are so convinced that punishment is always justified, and must reflect sin on the part of the sufferer. Therefore, they "know" that Job can end his suffering if only he will tell God he's sorry he's been such a sinner. The position of the "comforters" is that people can control God by their own right behavior. Job's position puts God in charge. Theirs puts humans in charge. By the end of the story, God confirms Job's argument that humans do not have the power of self-justification and rebukes the other men for their self-aggrandizement.

And now for the second time Job's wife is mentioned:, "My breath is repulsive to my wife." (19:17 NRSV) That his breath is repulsive is no surprise. Ill and depressed, Job has not been eating, a natural consequence of which is halitosis. But I think there's more to be gleaned from this about their relationship. Clearly she has been close enough to him to be offended by his breath, so we know he hasn't driven her away, literally or figuratively. And I also read into this an intimacy strong enough that she can come right out and tell him his breath is bad. I choose to see that kind of intimacy as an integral part of their relationship.

Finally, "If my heart has been enticed by a woman, and I have lain in wait at my neighbor's door, then let my wife grind for another, and let other men kneel over her. For that would be a heinous crime; that would be a criminal offense; for that would be a fire consuming down to Abaddon, and it would burn to the root all my harvest." (31: 9-12 NRSV)

If one really wanted to, one could find explanations – probably legalistic – of other meaning behind these words. But for me, it seems most simple and direct to accept this at face value – that he has been faithful to his wife. True, in the society of Job's time, he might have taken other wives or concubines, but it seems to me like a stretch to go beyond this simple statement of monogamy. I have chosen for my story to assume that Job and his wife respect and love each other.

Working since 1970 with secular textbooks and articles about women, I encountered an occasional reference to Proverbs 31:10-31, "Ode to a Capable Wife" (See Appendix). It has often been presented as a negative example of how hard a woman's life is. Women sometimes recognized it when I incorporated it into my talks, but Jewish women's groups always nodded in positive reaction to "the woman of valor."

As I thought about the women in my own extended family, I realized how many of my aunts fit the picture of this woman who is basically in charge of everything involved in daily life: buying, selling, merchandizing, traveling, dispensing charity, sharing wisdom, providing the necessities of food and warmth. And, unless they are living in dire poverty, these are the women who feel good about themselves, productive, useful, and respected. Depression was more likely to develop for women who were assigned a more dependent role in our culture.

I came to understand that the ideal wife in Proverbs 31 had an important function, and freed her husband to perform his, which was, at that time, to study, worship, and sacrifice to God. While the culture of the 1970s valued buying, selling, merchandizing, traveling, dispensing charity, sharing wisdom, and providing the necessities of food and warmth as primarily an honorable masculine function, to really understand women of the time of Proverbs 31, we had to understand the different culture. If Job, in standing respectfully before God, was an honorable Self–actualizer, then so was his wife as she went about her busy, productive life of tending to daily needs.

Now I knew I wanted to write the story of Job's wife, and I felt comfortable with the psychology of it. But this is a Biblical story, so I needed some confirmation from an appropriate scholar. I called Brevard Childs, the noted Old Testament scholar at Yale, and asked him if it would be appropriate to take the ideal wife of Proverbs 31 as a model for Mrs. Job. His answer was an unhesitating "yes." The book of Job and the "ideal wife" are both part of wisdom literature, probably from the patriarchal period. And he encouraged me to write it. Little could either one of us know how long it would be before Mrs. Job finally would be birthed.[7]

Professor Childs is not responsible for any of the other assumptions I've made in writing this story. He is, however, responsible for my developing the courage to write it. As I understand it, wisdom literature is exactly that – attempts to define and teach wisdom. It was for that reason that I chose to name Mrs. Job "Dara" (Wisdom). Equally in the running for a name was "Hope" which, I felt, reflected a particularly strong element of her personality, but perhaps hope is just one small part of wisdom, so Dara she is.

The book of Mrs. Job is fiction, but there are two areas where it has to be faithful to the source. First, while the interpretation of the particular events of the trials and their aftermath are mine, their depiction must be true to the Biblical story. Second, the details of their life must reflect the reality of the time in which they live.

My sister, the one in the family with the MFA in writing, has told me that one reads, takes notes on, and experiences a lot of material, but when it comes to writing fiction, all that serves as background against which the story is created. She finally helped free me of my academic perfectionist trap. Her final nudge was to give me a very attractive journal to be used only for writing about Mrs. Job. What follows is some of the background that informed Mrs. Job's story as I was freed to create it.

Essentially in my research I have found no scholar who claims that the book of Job is the description of a particular man, his friends and family, and the events of his life, though there may be those who believe in the literal inerrancy of the Bible who will disagree with me. I hope they too can enjoy whatever wisdom there is in my story of Mrs. Job. I have found scholars, however, who have made suggestions about Job's location in time and place, and some have suggested men of history who may have been models for the character Job. Since no one is really sure about Job's roots, what follows is a description of the choices I've made.

The Book of Job is part of wisdom literature, which includes Job, Proverbs, and Ecclesiastes in the Hebrew Bible. There is no definitive agreement on who wrote the

Book of Job, or even how many authors were involved, but a good guess is that the poet/author was writing somewhere between the 9th and 6th century BCE and may have placed the story as far back as 2200 BCE. There is general agreement that the Job of the story was an Edomite, or alternatively from Uz which is in the region of Edom. I have chosen to identify the Job of my story as an Edomite, because it gives me context for many aspects of my story.

The Edomites were semi-nomads who followed their herds in spring, summer, and autumn, and lived within a walled city in the winter. A characteristic of Edom as revealed by a search of the internet is that at least some of their city homes were in caves. Edom was located on the eastern side of what we call the Dead Sea, largely in an area which is now part of Jordan.

Choosing to identify Job as an Edomite helped define many other parts of Mrs. Job's story. Edom is another name for Esau, whose mother and younger twin brother, Jacob, basically cheated him of his father's blessing and the heritage that should have been his. (Genesis 27:1-40.) When Jacob fled to his Uncle Laban to escape Esau's wrath, Esau took as an additional wife the daughter of Ishmael, the son of Abraham by Hagar the Egyptian, Sarah's slave girl. He did that knowing it would offend his mother.

Choosing to accept the Edomite background for Job, then, opened up the possibility of understanding Job's piety as that of one converted to a lost faith – lost because of the heritage of anger and resentment. In the background of my thought, I see Eliphaz and the others, along with Job, recovering the God of Abraham and his sons Isaac, patriarch of the Jews, and Ishmael, patriarch of the Islamic faith.

Every bit as important in the story of Esau and Jacob as background for Job is the reconciliation that occurred, basically because of Esau's forgiveness, when Jacob returned with his family and flocks to the land of his father. As he approached Edom, the land in which Esau had settled, Esau met him with an embrace. (Genesis 33: 1-17.) Without the fact of that forgiveness and reconciliation, it would have been harder to portray the generosity and ultimate piety of Job.

The background for my assumptions about Job's heritage was aided even further by another exploration of the internet where I came upon NABATAEA.NET, "The Hyksos, Kings of Egypt and the land of Edom: Chapter IV: The Book of Job." (Most recently reviewed 8/17/07.)[8] Here the author proposes that Job is modeled on King Jobab, who, if I understand the author correctly, can trace his lineage back to Esau. Please understand that I am in no position to claim or dispute the accuracy of these assumptions, but they do allow me to embed my story in a reasonable framework. Here is the lineage. Esau fathered Ruel and Eliphaz (and King Bela?). Ruel fathered Zerah who fathered Jobab. In adopting this base for my story, I am, therefore, making Job the great grandson of Esau and a relative to Eliphaz.

But here's the wrinkle created by artistic preference, or something like that. I had almost finished the first draft when I realized that, to be true to this assumption, Job's father should have been Zerah, not Ruel as I had been calling him. So, I set my computer to work changing all the "Ruels" to "Zerah." Uncle Ruel was gone from my manuscript and instead there was this stranger, Uncle Zerah. Now I know what writers mean when they talk about identifying with their characters. Truly, I went into mourning over the loss of Uncle Ruel, whom I had come to love, and perceived Uncle Zerah as an undesirable intruder. After a conference with my writer sister, I concluded with her help that, since this is fiction, I could bring Uncle Ruel back – a great relief to me. Then Pastor Beth Warpmaeker, much to my delight, pointed out that Zerah would have been Ben Ruel (son of Ruel) so I can feel even more justified calling him Uncle Ruel for short.

Now you have a pretty detailed description of the choices I have made on the way to creating "The Book of Mrs. Job." I love Job and Dara. I also enjoy the issues of justice, self-justification, grace, and the masculinity/femininity of the deity. I am a psychologist, and it's mostly the psychological questions that drew me.

I have come to love the other characters in the book as well. Since they are largely my own creation, I guess that's a way of loving myself. So be it. They say that writers don't really create anything new, that they write about what they have experienced. Looking back at the story, I guess that says something either about my own positive experiences in life, my own optimism, or my own Pollyanna tendencies. Whatever the reason, I see that I haven't created even one mean and nasty person, except perhaps for the nameless attackers who brought on the trials.

I have also been pleased by the comment of Pastor Dave Olson of Mount Calvary Lutheran Church. He pointed out what the Hebrew tradition sees as the purpose of Biblical stories. It is to promote discussion in depth of the issues raised. I guess that's what Job was doing as he worshiped God, and I like to think that's what I am doing in seeing the story of Job in this particular way.

Please remember, I'm a psychologist, a therapist, maybe a writer, but not a theologian or a historian. I've just tried to get Mrs. Job's story right.

Previous publications by the author

When to Forgive
NEW HARBINGER PUBLICATIONS

Forgiving One Page at a Time
AUTHOR HOUSE

Mrs. Job
iUNIVERSE
Early edition of
"Figs & Pomegranates & Special Cheeses"

APPENDIX

Proverbs 31:10-31, Ode To A Capable Wife

A capable wife who can find?
She is far more precious than jewels.

The heart of her husband trusts in her,
and he will have no lack of gain.

She does him good, and not harm,
all the days of her life.

She seeks wool and flax,
and works with willing hands.

She is like the ships of the merchant,
she brings her food from far away.

She rises while it is still night and provides food for
her household and tasks for her servant girls.

She considers a field and buys it;
with the fruit of her hands she plants a vineyard.

She girds herself with strength,
and makes her arms strong.

She perceives that her merchandise is profitable.
her lamp does not go out at night.

She puts her hands to the distaff,
and her hands hold the spindle.

She opens her hand to the poor,
and reaches out her hands to the needy.

She is not afraid for her household when it snows,
for all her household are clothed in crimson.

She makes herself coverings,
her clothing is fine linen and purple.

Her husband is known in the city gates,
taking his seat among the elders of the land.

She makes linen garments and sells them;
she supplies the merchant with sashes.

Strength and dignity are her clothing,
and she laughs at the time to come.

She opens her mouth with wisdom,
and the teaching of kindness is on her tongue.

She looks well to the ways of her household,
and does not eat the bread of idleness.

Her children rise up and call her happy;
her husband too, and he praises her.

"Many women have done excellently,
but you surpass them all."

Charm is deceitful, and beauty is vain,
but a woman who fears the Lord is to be praised,

Give her a share in the fruit of her hands,
and let her works praise her in the city gates. (NRSV)

ENDNOTES

1. Jemimah is the name given to Job's oldest daughter in the biblical story.

2. Mitchell, Stephen. The Book of Job. San Francisco: North Point Press, 1987, p. 35.

3. Safire, William. The First Dissident: The Book of Job in Today's Politics. New York: Random House, 1992.

4. Dershowitz, Alan M. The Genesis of Justice: Ten Stories of Biblical Injustice that Led to the Ten Commandments as Modern Law. New York: Warner Books, 2000.

5. Safire, Op. Cit., p. 3. "In many translations, the definite article precedes the word Satan in the Old Testament, suggesting a title like Special Prosecutor, or Inspector General, rather than a person's name."

6. Pagels, Elaine. The Origin of Satan. New York: Random House, 1995, p. 39. "In the Hebrew Bible, as in mainstream Judaism to this day, Satan never appears as Western Christendom has come to know him, as the leader of an 'evil empire,' an army of hostile spirits who make war on God and human kind alike. As he first appears in the Hebrew Bible, Satan is not necessarily evil, much less opposed to God. On the contrary, he appears in the book of Numbers and in Job as one of God's obedient servants—a messenger, or angel ...152 In biblical sources, the Hebrew term the satan describes an adversarial role. It is not the name of a particular character."

   Taylor, Barbara Brown. "Who are the Bad Guys?" Christian Century. May 3, 2003: 43. "Minus one cryptic reference in 1 Chronicles, Satan first appears in the Book of Job, where he works as God's prosecuting attorney. Satan cannot do anything to Job that God will not let him do. When Job's children are killed, they are killed with God's permission. When sores erupt on Job's body, they erupt with God's permission. As hard as this is for Job or his readers to swallow, it is one of the occupational hazards of monotheism. There is "only one God in this story—the God who forms light and creates darkness, according to Isaiah 45—the God who makes weal and creates woe."

7. I have been saddened to learn of Dr. Child's death in the summer of 2007.

8. http://www.nabataea.net/, Gibson, David J. "The Hyksos, Kings of Egypt and the land of Edom: Chapter IV: The Book of Job" (most recently reviewed 8/17/07).